CRAZY ABOUT YOUR LOVE 2

CHANIQUE J

ACKNOWLEDGMENTS

I'm going to start by thanking God as always. Without him, all of this wouldn't be possible. It takes a lot to actually start and complete a book and I'm grateful to have the gift of doing so. My number one priority and source of motivation comes from my son, Ke-Chan. The joy he gets from being able to show people his name in a book brings a smile to my face! To my family, I want you all to know how much your love and support means to me. All of the love and support from my friends is an amazing feeling. There are some friends I've been separated from and the support they show me has brought us back together and I am forever grateful for that.

I'm trying to keep this as short and simple as possible without forgetting anyone, so please forgive me in advance. Thank you to all of my fans and supporters; you guys just don't know how much it means to me! I appreciate all the love you give me. As long as yawl rocking with me and showing support, I'm going to continue to keep the books coming. Last but certainly not least, I have to thank my publisher, Shan! I could write a paragraph alone on you and how much of a blessing you have been to me. Just know I appreciate you and everyone on our team! I know after part one yawl are more than ready for what's next, so I'll leave this here and just say enjoy! Keep your eyes open for my next book!

Sincerely,

Chaniqué J.

The love shared between Lee and Coby was undeniably one of a kind. The type of love you never want to get over. When things took a turn for the worst in part one, will Coby be willing to mend Lee's broken heart and work past their differences? Coby has changed in his eyes for the better, while Lee believes it's for the worst when his deepest secrets are revealed.

Finally, Renee and Dupree take the time to allow their relationship to grow and it becomes too hard of a pill for Mark to swallow. Even with a life outside of Renee and starting a family of his own, he still feels the need to resurface in Renee's love life. How will Renee respond? Will she leave the past where it is or will she play with fire? Dupree is a pretty good guy, but is he too good to be true?

Erin, Dame, and Kena have a love triangle of their own. You would've thought Dame learned his lesson the first time around messing with these messy broads, but I guess once isn't enough. The grass isn't always greener on the other side as they say.

No matter what secrets, lies, and truth were revealed in part one, will the storms be enough to stop the couples from being crazy about the love they share?

Table of Content

I had been anticipating this day for the past month or so. It was finally the last day I would see this place, hopefully ever, but I was still unsure since I hadn't received my letter of acceptance for the fall semester at Ohio State University. Summer break was something I'd looked forward to. There was no way in hell I planned on taking any summer courses; I needed a break from class, tests, and homework.

Ending my freshman year with straight A's and landing on the Dean's List, I was more than proud of myself. I had already packed all of my belongings that I would be taking back home with me over the past week and it was now time for me to hit the road. It was a bittersweet feeling to actually be leaving West Virginia. Rod and I had become so close and I was going to miss him so much over this break, but he promised to come visit me once he was done with the two-week internship he landed with the city.

On the other hand, I was happy as hell to be leaving Kelly. Yeah, I dropped the problem we had before spring break, but I still didn't like living with her snake ass. After that one incident, I no longer trusted her, nor wanted to be around her. My last final was on a Tuesday morning so instead of leaving Thursday as I originally planned, I was taking off today. If I didn't have to stay here a minute longer, I wasn't going to.

I hadn't told anyone I was coming home early. Like always, my first stop would be to see Coby. Since I didn't leave West Virginia until after five o'clock, it was already starting to get dark outside. I couldn't wait to see the look on Coby's face when I surprised him with my early arrival. I planned on dedicating this entire summer to fixing the strained relationship I had created between Coby and me. My main focus would be my man and nothing else.

Instead of carrying all my bags inside tonight, I would just grab them tomorrow morning. When I put my key in the door, I made sure to open and close it as quietly as possible. I didn't want him to hear me so I tiptoed upstairs and when I heard moaning, I assumed Coby was watching porn as always. Coby had developed a weird ass fascination with porn, and as bad as I disliked it, that was his thing so I never said anything.

When I busted through the bedroom door, I was immediately sick to my stomach. I couldn't hold back my tears or the food I had earlier for lunch. Witnessing the love of my life balls deep in a fuckin' man that looked like a woman crushed me to my soul. If it wasn't for me seeing the long skinny dick hanging low, I would've never known it was another man Coby was fuckin'. How could he do this to me? How could he be in the room he claims we shared, fucking someone else? Another man at that.

"Lee, what the fuck are you doing here?" Coby yelled, jumping up from the position he was in and racing towards me.

I hadn't prepared myself for what was going to happen next because I was still throwing up. More like dry heaving because I had emptied out my stomach when I first opened the door. Instead of explaining himself and consoling me, Coby started punching me with all his might and fighting me as if I was a stranger on the street that had just broken into his home.

"Why the fuck would you just bust in and pop up on me unannounced, bitch! You better not mention a word of this to any fucking body, do you hear me?"

I couldn't even answer his question because I was screaming at the top of my lungs for him to stop and to get off of me. The he-she Coby was just balls deep in must have felt bad watching him beat the shit out of me because he was now pulling Coby off of me, telling him to calm down and stop. I wasn't in any way happy that the "it" was here, but I was thankful that he was able to save me from the worst ass beating I had gotten in my entire life.

I struggled to get up on my feet and ran to my car. I left Coby's front door wide open, not worried about anything else besides getting the fuck out of there as quickly as possible. I was shaken and beaten bloody, so I couldn't go to my parents' house. The first person I thought to contact was my sister, Renee. I hopped on the nearest freeway to head to her house and it started pouring down raining. As if it wasn't hard enough to see with a swollen eye from Coby's beating, I was crying and attempting to text Renee and let her know I was on my way to her house. I got a text from Coby after hitting send on the message to Renee.

Coby: Just because you left just now doesn't mean you're leaving me. Lee, I don't care what you saw or how you feel about this, we are not over and if I can't have you then no one will.

Before I could put my phone back between my legs I heard a loud horn coming from a semi-truck behind me. I tried to swerve back into the lane I was previously in but it was too late. With the road being wet and slippery, I swerved and lost control of the wheel. I felt the first hit and my car began to tumble. My head was playing ping pong, hitting different areas of my car. I felt another hard impact and my car came to a complete stop, but not before the airbag burst out of my steering wheel and hit me in the face. Right when I thought the impact was over, I felt an even larger boom and blood trickling down my face.

"God, please help me and..."

Before I could finish my prayer, everything went black...

Walking into the emergency room of the University Hospital Main Campus was the last thing I expected to be doing in the middle of the night when I laid my head down for the evening. Seeing my parents pacing the floors with shared worried expressions caused me to get a sick feeling in the pit of my stomach. My mom called me and told me that Lee, my little sister, my right hand, my rollie, and best friend had been in a severe car accident. From the sound of my mother's voice, I could tell she was a nervous wreck, which put me in even more of a panic. I received the call from my mom not even twenty minutes ago and the twenty-five-minute commute to the hospital from my house was cut short with me speeding to get here, leaving Sanai at the house with Dupree. I didn't intentionally leave them but I was so caught off guard by the call that the only thing that came to mind was to get to my sister's side. I didn't even know Lee was in Ohio. She wasn't due to return back home until Thursday evening and today is Tuesday, so what the fuck is really going on.

"Renee, my baby! My baby, Renee!" my mother cried, reaching out for my embrace. The hurt she felt inside was apparent on her face.

"What happened, mommy? How did it happen? When did she get here? Where did it happen exactly?" I questioned my mom. It wasn't intentional to ask so many questions all at once, it's just I was so confused and I needed answers at the moment.

"I don't know, baby. I don't know anything right now. I know just as little as you do. When I got the call that my baby had been in a car accident and that I needed to get to the hospital as soon as possible, I called you as soon as I hung up the phone," my mother stated with tears still streaming down her face. My dad was still pacing the floor and hadn't spoken a word. The look of worry was written on his forehead in all capital letters. My dad had never been the type of man to show his emotions, so to see him so worried and nervous, I knew things had to have been pretty bad. When I saw my dad walking towards the opposite direction, I turned to see Kris running into the emergency room with Dame on his heels.

"Family of Lanice Johns?" a tall Asian doctor stated while scanning the crowded emergency room waiting area for a response. We all eagerly rushed toward him, anxious for the news he had to break to us.

"How is she?" my mother asked with pleading eyes as if she was begging him to deliver good news and not the worst.

"Hello, I'm Dr. Wang. I'm the physician that was called to operate on Ms. Johns upon her arrival and I'll get straight to the point for you. I won't lie, Ms. Johns is in pretty bad shape. She's fortunate enough to still be with us after the accident she was in. There are several broken bones throughout her entire body, including her face. In order to operate on Ms. Johns, we were forced to medically sedate her so she is sleeping at the moment. She won't be waking up for quite a few hours, but she will live. However, the road to recovery will not be short, nor an easy one for her. Once we have her moved to a recovery room a nurse will be back to inform you. She is able to have two visitors at a time and I'm sure it won't be much longer before you guys can head back. If you guys have any questions, again, my name is Dr. Wang," the doctor stated while reaching out to shake my mom and dad's hands before turning around and heading back where he came from.

I could hear my dad let out a sigh of relief, yet he still wore the same worried expression on his face. My mom, on the other hand, was kneeled down on her hands and knees, praying in the middle of the emergency room. Kris and Dame took a seat and I could tell that they were in dire need of a blunt to ease their minds. Shit, if I could smoke without worrying about being randomly drug tested by my job, I would have encouraged it at the moment. As I took a seat next to Kris, Dupree was entering the visitors waiting area.

"What's going on, is she ok?" Dupree asked as he took a seat next to me and wrapped his arms around my shoulder. It's almost like his embrace was all I was waiting for to break down. As I explained to Dupree everything the doctor had just shared with us, I couldn't stop the tears from flowing. After updating him on all the information I had to offer, I said a silent prayer, asking God to be with not only my sister but the entire family, and for a speedy recovery. Even though the doctor said she would make it, I still wouldn't feel at ease until my sister woke up and I could see her for myself.

"Where is Sanai?" I softly spoke, asking Dupree after finally realizing I had left my daughter with him and she wasn't here with us.

"I dropped her off to my pops before coming here. I didn't know exactly what happened or what was going on so I figured that would be best for her," Dupree stated and I was thankful he was thinking in his right mind because I damn sure wasn't. I hadn't even texted or called to inform Erin, Netia, or Coby of what was going on. Since I didn't have Coby's number to contact him, I would have to wait until I received Lee's personal belongings. That's if they were able to retrieve them from the scene. I sent Erin and Netia a quick text letting them know Lee had been in a car accident and what hospital we were all at.

After about thirty minutes of waiting for a nurse to come give us the ok to go back and visit Lee, I was finally walking down the hall in the direction of the room with my mom to see Lee. When we reached room 308, I took a deep breath before opening the door. I know the doctor said that Lee was pretty bad but I wasn't expecting to see her this bad off. If I wouldn't have been with my mother, I don't know if I would have been able to hold it together. Lee's beautiful face was extremely swollen and almost unidentifiable. Her eyes were closed due to her being asleep, but even if she was awake they would've been swollen shut because they were so big. She had two black eyes and her jaw was extremely big and looked a little odd. I prayed for her sake that her jaw was not broken. There were machines everywhere and IV's leading to both arms. Lee had dried up blood on her face and neck. My mom couldn't do anything besides cry and call for God to help her child. I can't even imagine how she feels at the moment. Instead of saying anything, I just stood by her side and rubbed her back to console her the best I could. After my mom rubbed Lee's hand and said a prayer with her, she told me she would be back once she informed my father of how she was doing. My dad and Kris both opted to stay in the waiting area. Seeing Lee in this type of condition and not being able to help her would have driven the two of them into a rage that wouldn't be able to be tamed. There wasn't anyone in particular for them to take it out on, so pacing the floor in the waiting room was best for both of them.

The nurse came in and gave me what little belongings of Lee's they were able to retrieve from the scene, which wasn't much. I'm thankful that there wasn't a lock code set on her phone so I was able to access her phone book, then contact those closest to her and inform them of her condition. Lee had several missed calls from not only Coby but her male best friend, Rod, as well. Although I had only personally met Rod face to face once at her game, I felt the need to reach out to him to inform him because of the closeness they shared, but that would be after I called Coby. When I called Coby back he didn't answer, so I sent him a quick text letting him know it was me and that Lee had been in a bad car accident and was in the hospital. Calling Rod, I felt bad because it was damn near three o'clock in the morning and the average person would be sleep, but under these unfortunate circumstances we weren't. When Rod answered the phone I could tell he was sleeping by his raspy tone.

"Hey, Rod, this is Renee, Lee's older sister. I'm calling you because I see she had several missed calls from you but she wasn't able to answer or return any of your calls because she was involved in a bad car accident and we are at the hospital now."

"Wait, what? Is she ok? What hospital are you guys at?" Rod asked, sounding as if he had awakened completely after hearing the news.

"She's pretty bad off but the doctors are expecting her to make it. She is sleep right now and has been since the surgery. We are at the

Ohio State University Hospital on Campus," I managed to say all in one breath, allowing my tears to fall freely.

"Ok! I'm getting up now. I'll be there as soon as possible. Please keep me updated on any changes that may occur before I get there." I could hear Rod moving things around in his background, sounding as if he was in a hurry and now up out of bed.

"Are you coming all the way to Columbus right now?" I asked, a little shocked by his sense of urgency to be here with her.

"Yeah, I am, soon as I get dressed. Will you have her phone?"

"Yes, I'll have her phone."

"Coo', I'll call you as soon as I'm getting off the freeway near the hospital for the room number. Thank you, Renee, and try to think positive. Lee is strong; she's going to be just fine. Try not to worry yourself too much. She needs you to be strong in order for her to be strong." If only I could take Rod's words and put them into action. It was easier said than done to be strong at the moment because of the way Lee looked. Although I wasn't sitting in her room any longer, I could still see the image of my little sister laying there helplessly. Lee had never been hurt to the point where she needed to be hospitalized, so this was a hard pill to swallow.

Hearing that Rod was about to get out of his bed in the middle of the night to drive three and a half hours to be by Lee's side showed me just how much he loved my sister. I'm glad she has a friend in her corner that cares enough about her to do something like that. I'm sure once Coby finds out he will be here as well, but I honestly don't want to see his ass. Yeah, Coby is Lee's boyfriend and I know she loves him unconditionally, but I can sense that nigga is foul. I'm just waiting for it to come out to the light. I respect him on the strength of the love my sister has for him, but the way he's been acting lately reminded me so much of Mark, and I can't stand that shit. Lee hasn't told me anything negative about Coby but I can feel it in my soul that that man is doing my sister wrong. My mom also feels he's up to some shit and not doing right by Lee. Yeah, my mom keeps her mouth closed and stays out of our business for the most part, but she slides her little remarks in here and there, throwing shade. She also put me in on her little secret about putting a ton of Ex-lax in Coby's German chocolate cake she baked for him a few weeks back. When she told me that shit I damn near shitted on myself from laughing so hard, picturing the outcome. Lee hadn't mentioned it so I'm taking it Coby didn't know the reason for his sudden diarrhea. I know his big greedy ass ate it all without any thought just because he's always been a fan of my mom's cooking. That is the exact reason why you don't eat everyone's food, especially without knowing how they really feel about you.

I hadn't realized I had dozed off until I felt the vibration from Lee's phone that was placed on my lap. Seeing that the caller ID displayed that it was Rod, I hurried and pressed the green button, connecting our call.

"Hello?"

"Hey, Renee, sorry to wake you! I'm pulling into the hospital main parking garage now. What floor are you guys on?"

"You're fine. I didn't even know I had fallen asleep until I felt the phone going off, but we are on the 3rd floor in the waiting area."

"Ok, thanks, I'll see you in a second."

"Ok." Ending our call, I glanced around the waiting area to see a sleeping Erin, Netia, Dame and Kris huddled in the corner. My dad was watching the news as if he was well rested, but I knew he hadn't been to sleep. Dupree must've gone to the restroom because his jacket was laid across the seat next to me, but he wasn't anywhere in sight. When I turned my head in the opposite direction I was surprised to see Coby sitting in the corner with his attention fixed on his phone. He wasn't here before I drifted off to sleep, so my guess was he had just gotten here as well. He must've called my mom or dad because I didn't leave any specific information on our exact whereabouts in the text I sent him. Right as I shifted in my seat, I heard the elevator chime and witnessed a very stressed looking Rod rushing in my direction. The elevator must have gotten Coby's attention as well because he looked up and eyed Rod when he came over to me.

"Hey, Renee, how are you? Are there any updates on Lee?"

"Hey, Rod. No, there hasn't been any just yet. My mom is back there with her because after visiting hours, she is only allowed to have one person stay with her in the room. I'm sure my mom is awake and won't mind coming out so you can sneak back and see her if you would like to."

"Nah, I'm fine. I'll just sit out here with you guys until either she comes out or visiting hours start back up in a few hours."

"Ok, well if you change your mind just let me know and I can call her cell phone. Oh, Rod, by the way, we appreciate you coming all the way up here to be here for Lee. Not many friends would do something like that," I told Rod, and I meant every word of it.

"It's no problem. Thank you for calling me. Lee knows I got her back no matter what. There's no way I could've gone back to sleep and stayed in West Virginia without knowing she was ok and seeing her for myself. Not saying your words aren't good enough, but I needed to be here and physically see her." I could tell from the sincerity in his voice that Rod was one hundred about every word he spoke concerning my sister.

No matter how hard I tried to remain focused and get through my entire work shift without slipping up on my responsibilities, I couldn't help but think about Lee and what she told me when she woke up a few days ago. As bad as I wanted to share the information she told me, I made a promise to her that I would keep everything between us two, especially since I was the only person she trusted well enough to tell her secret to. I didn't want her to regret ever opening up to me about what had been going on in her personal life. I knew Coby was up to some foul shit but I would've never believed that Coby had been putting his hands on Lee and she was allowing it. Lee is normally a fire-cracker and willing to fuck someone up at the drop of a dime. Then again, I guess love will make you do shit you would've never expected. With Coby being Lee's first love, I can understand why it's hard for her to just walk away and not leave him. Lee explained to me how Coby kicked her ass when she popped up to surprise him at his house and caught him in a compromising position with another man. Now, hearing that was mind blowing. I couldn't do shit but shake my head when she said that. The fact that Coby was fucking a nigga on the low while still messing around with my little sister at the same time enraged me, but I had to keep my cool for the sake of it being Lee's secret. Not only was he low down and dirty for doing the shit, but he could've contracted any type of disease and passed it right on along to innocent ol' Lee. Being cheated on is one thing, but to be cheated on with another man had to make Lee feel some type of way on the inside and like less of a woman, but now was not the time to dwell on that when her physical health was more important. Our number one priority at the moment is her health; we can face all this other drama and stress once she gets better. Lee suffered two broken legs, several fractured ribs, a broken wrist, a fractured collar bone, and she had a small fracture in her jawline. Those were only some of the injuries she sustained during the car accident. Lee also had burns from the airbag on her arm and face, with two black eyes and a broken nose. I'm sure Coby was responsible for some of the damage that was done, but Lee didn't specify how much damage he caused with his latest beating. Lee and I allowed everyone to believe all of her injuries came from the car accident that followed after leaving Coby's place. When Lee disclosed everything to me, she requested that we limit her visitors to only immediate family, with the exception of Rod. Lee made it clear that Coby wasn't allowed, nor did she want Coby to find out that anyone outside of family was allowed. I'm glad Lee was willing to allow Rod to see her in this condition because he had traveled all the way from West Virginia to Ohio, putting his very own life on hold to be by her side in her time of need. Lee is supposed to be released from the hospital next week, but will have to take physical therapy for a few months once her three cast are removed to ensure she is recovering properly.

On top of the mental stress from worrying about Lee and work, Mark had been harassing the shit out of me. It's almost like he wasn't getting the point that we were over and he didn't know when to leave well enough alone. Mark continued with the constant calls or texts about Sanai and how he needed his own proof that she didn't belong to him. Yeah, Dupree and I have the copies of the paternity test that indicated that Dupree was in fact 99.9% the father of Sanai, but that wasn't for the sake of Mark's personal preference. The fact that I was willing to make myself look bad and admit to my fault of saying she was his all this time should've been enough. I didn't and still don't feel it's necessary to share Mark's stupidity with Dupree because he has enough going on with his own life outside of being a great father and boyfriend. Dupree hasn't moved in with Sanai and me as of yet, but one would never know because he's with us more than he's at his own place. We are finally together and I'm happy to say things are going good between us. I refuse to allow Mark's possessive ass ways to be the reason that things start to become shaky between the two of us. Dupree is a great father. It's almost like being a father comes naturally for Dupree. You would never guess that Sanai is his first and only child from the way he acts with her. Sanai doesn't even seem to miss Mark one little bit; she hasn't asked for him or cried out randomly. Sanai has even begun to call Dupree dad, so it's almost as if she's known all along. Dupree's father is just as bad as my parents when it comes to trying to hog Sanai; he wants her over with him all the time. Dupree's dad says that Sanai is the daughter he never had and spoils the mess out of her. It's safe to say that little girl is beyond spoiled rotten. It's her way or no way and I don't exactly know who to place the blame on. Sanai has been doing great outside of the one incident we had. We haven't had to make any more trips to the hospital regarding her sickle cell, thank God. Now as far as her behavior, that's a whole 'nother story. She is so busy now that she is up and walking; I feel like I'm raising two kids instead of one. Even with the help of Dupree and my parents, I'm still extremely tired, so I could only imagine how hard it would be if I had to raise her alone.

Taking me out of my thoughts, I realized that it was finally the end of my shift and I'll be damn if no sooner than I powered on my phone, I had six unread text messages from Mark.

Mark: Why you not answering my calls?

Mark: I'm 'bout to just start popping up since you want to be childish and keep my daughter away from me!

Mark: Bitch since you want to be spiteful I'm going to act just as simple as you are acting.

Mark: I bet if I call up to your job you'll answer my calls then.

Mark: It must be that nigga in your ear that got you acting all brand new.

Mark: You going to make me fuck you and that nigga up just wait and see.

Instead of replying to him, I closed the messages just as quickly as I opened them. Of all the times, now is not the time for him to be bothering me with his bullshit. I have more than enough on my plate and chaos going on in my life at the moment, so adding his drama is completely unnecessary. As soon as I pick up Sanai from daycare I'm heading to Dupree's father's house to drop her off before heading back up to the hospital to check on Lee, then home I go so I can prepare dinner for the night. Since I'm off tomorrow, Dupree's dad is keeping Sanai tonight so I can get up and spend the entire day at the hospital with Lee, without my busy body one-year-old tagging along. As bad as my parents wanted to protest about not going to the hospital in the morning, they needed to sleep in and catch up on some much-needed rest. Going to the hospital bright and early every morning and staying majority of the day had become a ritual for the two of them. Since Lee's car accident, the two of them have been a nervous wreck. Even though Lee is progressing, their levels of stress haven't gone down any.

By the time I reached the hospital, Mark had called my cell phone another ten times and left a voicemail message each and every time I ignored his call. Then to top it off he sent five text messages back to back as well. After reading the first one where he threatened to come by my house and not only fuck me up but Dupree as well, I placed his number on the block list. There is no way I can deal with his continued disrespect and ignorant behavior.

Walking into Lee's hospital room, I wasn't the least bit surprised to see Rod sitting in the corner of the room, keeping her company. That man had been here by her side just as much as my mother. You would have thought that he was Lee's boyfriend instead of her best friend. I can only imagine the types of strings he had to pull in order to up and come to Columbus on such short notice, then he will be staying here even after she is discharged. Yeah, that's right, Lee told me that Rod told her he would be staying here in Columbus until she had a full recovery in order to take the load off of my parents some. Not only did Lee appreciate his help and support, but my family did as well. Rod didn't know just how much of a load he was taking off of all of us just by being here. Lee also said something about Rod having family here so he was familiar with the city and felt comfortable sticking around longer, which was great. My family treats him with great hospitality, but there's nothing like being near your own family.

"Hey, sister! How are you feeling today!" I happily greeted Lee.

"Hey, Nae. I'm still in pain but better than yesterday. Every day is the same but a little better than the day before. I know one thing, I'm so sick of being in this hospital, though, I can tell you that. They swear they want you to get your rest so you can heal, yet they in my face every damn minute talking about they are only checking my vitals or some shit," Lee said while attempting to adjust herself on the bed. I couldn't help but let out a slight chuckle because even with the situation she was in, Lee was still the same old Lee, with her feisty ass. I'm glad she wasn't allowing any of the things going on to mess with her spirits.

"I know you are tired of being here but they are only doing their job, Lee. It will be over soon, but I don't know if being back home with mom and dad will be any better," I started laughing.

"Shit, you're right, I didn't even think about it like that. I'm damned if I do and damned if I don't! I guess I better get used to this type of treatment until I'm able to get up and do shit on my own then. Right?"

"Yeah, you better, but don't rush it, Lee. Take your time so everything heals properly," I warned her in a concerned manner.

"Yeah, your sister is right, Lee. Just relax!" Rod spoke up and agreed with me.

"Thanks, Rod, 'cause she obviously thinks that she can do what she wants." We all let out a little laugh to lighten the mood some.

"I know yawl, I know! Dang! Well enough about me, where is my baby? I haven't got the chance to see her yet since I've been in this damn hospital. I know I'm all fucked up but damn, Nae! You do know that she is fifty percent my baby too, right?" Lee was referring to Sanai. Lee swore that Sanai was her child as well, and if you didn't personally know us you would think that because of the love Lee had for her niece.

"She's over Dupree's dad's house. He is keeping her for the night so I can come straight here in the morning. I know you want to see her Lee but Sanai is just busy as hell and the hospital is not the place I want to deal with her turning out. I promise I'll bring her up here soon though just so you can shut up crying." Lee playfully threw a piece of ice at me and turned her attention to her phone when it started vibrating on the side of her. The look on her face hinted at who was calling. It could have only been Coby. He was the only person that caused Lee to become uneasy as of late. I didn't know if Lee had shared with Rod the situations that were taking place between Coby and herself so I didn't say anything to her about her sudden mood change. I just turned my attention to my phone when she answered Coby's call. Rod also took the hint and whispered to me that he was heading out to return a few calls he had missed.

Lee's entire mood changed after speaking on the phone with Coby. It's like he caused a depression to sweep over her now. I didn't have the words to say to her because although Mark kicked my ass a few times, I wasn't in her exact situation. Everyone is so quick to pass judgment on the next person until it's them in the other person's shoes. Lee looked as if she had the world on her shoulders after that call. I wish I could take off some of the load she was carrying, but this is a situation Lee has to handle on her own in order to get over it completely. Until she is ready to talk, I just want her to have all the space mentally she may need.

"Lee, I know now isn't the time to talk but I will let you know if you ever need me I'm here. Whether it's a listening ear, advice, or physically. You are my sister and there isn't a thing that I wouldn't do for you. I love you and just know that no matter how you feel or whatever you choose to do, whether I agree with you or not, I have your back one hundred percent."

"Thanks, Nae. I really appreciate it. I love you too and that means a lot. I needed to hear that right about now." Rod was reentering the room as soon as Lee closed her mouth.

"Am I interrupting something? Should I go back out?" Rod asked, sensing the tension in the room and looking between Lee and me.

"No, you're fine, I'm actually about to leave. I was only stopping by for a few minutes. My parents are on their way up here anyways so you can go get some rest if you like." I grabbed my purse and kissed Lee on her forehead before rubbing her arm and walking towards the door.

"Love you, Nae. See you in the morning," Lee stated before shifting back some to get comfortable. I'm guessing the sudden sleepiness was the result of her medication beginning to kick in.

"Alright, Renee, be careful. I'll see you tomorrow as well," Rod said while waving bye in my direction.

"Love you too, Lee, and I sure will, Rod." I waved back as I exited the room.

Dinner was more than great and Dupree ended up switching things up on me when tonight was supposed to be all about him. The little stuff Dupree did to cater to me made me fall for him more and more each day. He had my bath water ran by the time I finished cleaning the few dishes after eating dinner. Lasagna, Caesar salad, garlic bread, and cheesecake couldn't have been a better choice of meal for today. We both ate our meal as if we hadn't eaten in weeks. I chose lasagna because that's one of Dupree's favorite meals and since today was supposed to be all about me making up to him for the lack of quality time spent lately, it was a perfect choice. The warm water felt amazing on my body; I hadn't realized how tense I was until now. Dupree showered before we ate so I knew he wouldn't be joining me. Instead of laying back in the warm bubbles to relax like he planned for me, I grabbed my washcloth and lathered my lavender body scrub onto my body. I wanted to make sure every crease of my body was clean because tonight was going to be eventful.

Once I dried off, I oiled my entire body, hitting all of my hotspots with my new Chanel No. 5 perfume, courtesy of Dupree as well. Instead of putting on lingerie, I chose to rock only my birthday suit and surprise Dupree. When I walked into the room, Dupree was laid out on the bed in only his Ralph Lauren boxer briefs and matching socks, watching SportsCenter. I sashayed into the bedroom and the look on his face was priceless. I could tell not only from the way he was eyeing me, licking his lips seductively and the bulge growing in his boxer briefs that he was enjoying his view.

I gave him a slight smirk and seductively crawled toward him on the bed. Grabbing for the waistline on his briefs, Dupree lifted his pelvic area up to assist me with removing the little clothing he did have on. Instead of wasting any time I got straight to the point. Licking my lips and gently taking the tip of his thick mushroom shaped head into my mouth, I prepared myself for the head I was about to deliver him. Dupree sat up on his elbows and looked down at me. Instead of giving him a side view of my ass, I positioned myself between his legs and faced him, all while keeping the tip of his dick in my warm mouth. I placed my hands on both sides of him and began to bob up and down slowly, allowing my saliva to coat his entire dick before I went any further. Once I realized his entire dick was coated with my saliva, I began to use my jaws as a suction, then started moving my head in a circular motion, all while moving up and down. I could tell he was feeling it because of the light moans he allowed to escape his lips. Speeding up the pace, I dropped down completely, taking him in entirely, allowing my throat to close in on the tip and humming before coming back up for air. "Shit... baby! Damn, you sucking that dick good as fuck. Ummmm...yeah, keep sucking that muthafucka like you want this dick." Dupree grabbed the back of my head and that's all I needed to hear before I started going hard as hell, deep throating him, slurping, slobbering, and humming as fast as I could. "Umm hum, you make me wanna turn your ass around and eat the fuck outta that pussy... Is that what you want, baby? You want daddy to eat the pussy, huh?" I looked up into his eyes as I dropped down to the base of his dick, before responding. Once my lips were practically touching his balls I hummed, "Umm hum." He pulled back so fast and flipped me over on my back before I could even protest. Spreading my legs as far apart as they would go, he took my clit into his mouth and started sucking. I felt the tingling sensation, causing my body to jerk. I reached to grab the back of his head and he reached up to encourage me to hold onto him. Holding his head, I started grinding my hips upward in a circular motion, bringing my orgasm even closer.

"Ohhh, damn this feels so good baby. I'mmm... I'mmm 'bout to cum." Dupree started licking and sucking on my clit faster when I gave the warning of my orgasm being near. I couldn't believe I was about to cum and he hadn't even been down there for two minutes yet. Feeling my legs stiffen up and shake simultaneously, I knew the end was near. The grip I had on his head was like I was holding him for dear life. I could hear Dupree sucking and slurping up all of my juices as they poured out of me. While still up on the high of my orgasm, Dupree sat up and slid his hard dick inside of me. No matter how many times we had sex, I still tensed up whenever he entered me. There was no way I could ever get one hundred percent used to a dick that big. He grabbed the arch of each of my feet with his hands and massaged them while delivering slow, yet steady strokes. The sounds of our love making and moans caused me to climax again.

"I love you, daddy."

"I love you too, baby." It was about to be a long night and I'm glad we sent Sanai to her grandpa's for the night because there was no way in hell one round of this would be enough. "Don't stop, daddy. I'm cumming, baby, I'm cumming." Just like that, I was having yet another orgasm.

I had been in this fucking hospital for too damn long if you ask me and my release day couldn't have come any sooner. It seems like as soon as the doctors were ready to release me, I had another obstacle come along each and every time, but today is the day I can finally go home. If it wasn't one thing, it was another. Thank God things were finally going in my favor for now. I hate attending physical therapy but in order to get discharged, I have to participate. Physical therapy made me want to collapse and go to sleep right after each and every session. Although I promised to attend every physical therapy session upon being discharged, I planned on doing the shit on my own. It's not that I can't do the task they ask of me, I just can't stand for a person to be in my face repeating themselves and trying to pretend they understand my frustration or my pain when they aren't in my shoes. Nobody knows how the fuck it feels to go from being a starting basketball player to now being overly excited just to learn to walk again with one fucking arm to use for assistance. Granted, my casts were finally off, but it still seemed like I was walking on noodles. It's not like I was ever a big person to begin with but those casts caused my legs to become even smaller than before. Being in the condition I am in and being in the hospital caused me to lose so much weight. As soon as the doctor brings in my discharge papers I'm wheeling my damn self downstairs to the lobby. I'm not sitting another minute in this room. My parents allowed Erin to come pick me up from the hospital since they had Sanai and Renee was at work. Rod offered to pick me up but he would have had to rush from doing something with his sister and that wouldn't be right. I felt like he had already done more than enough to help me and be here for me so there was no way I would insist on him going out of his way, just to come to my rescue once again if I had other options. I was happy that Rod had family here in Columbus to occupy some of his time because he had been at the hospital every day like he was the one in an accident. Shit, I was beginning to feel sorry for him. I felt like I had already been a huge inconvenience to his life, so I refused to have him stop what he was doing to pick me up. Instead, I told him he could come over to my parents' house later and chill for a second. My family wanted to do a welcome home party and have everyone over but honestly, I wasn't in the mood. It's not like I didn't see everyone on the regular. That's one thing I cannot complain about; the amount of visitors, attention and love everyone showed me was amazing. Coby even made several attempts to come visit me but I refused his visits and only accepted his calls so he wouldn't start his nonsense. In the beginning, I ignored his calls as well, but that only seemed to upset him more. After the stunt he pulled, I didn't know what Coby was capable of doing, nor did I want to find out.

"Ms. Johns, are you ready to get out of here finally and get back to your busy life?" The doctor came into the room with my discharge papers in hand, with my nurse following right behind him.

"Yes, you just don't know how happy I am to be leaving here, and all in one piece," I replied back in a joking manner, but meant every word of what I said.

"Now, Ms. Johns, you do still have to take it easy. Don't try to rush back to your normal activities once I discharge you. Remember everything we discussed and worked on while you were here as well. It is imperative that you make sure to attend those physical therapy sessions we set up for you in addition to your other discharge instructions. All the information is listed on your discharge papers but if you have any questions, concerns, or troubles, feel free to contact me here at the hospital or my office."

"I know and trust me, I will be doing as told. I'm not trying to slow up my recovery by being hard headed. Nor am I trying to end up right back in this place for not following your orders. I'm going to head downstairs to wait for my sister in the lobby if that's fine. She's pulling the car around," I lied. Erin hadn't even pulled up yet and I know that because she had already texted me letting me know she would be at least another ten minutes because the traffic and construction around the hospitals was a mess.

"Yeah, that's fine. I'll have your nurse, Cheryl, here wheel you down at least and you can go from there if you like. Take care, Ms. Johns."

"Yes, that's fine and thanks again for all you have done for me while here," I said while releasing the lock on the wheels of my wheelchair, eagerly attempting to leave this depressing ass room the moment he was out the door.

When the elevator chimed letting us know we were arriving on the first floor and lobby, I advised my nurse she could head back upstairs and I no longer needed her help from here. I was thankful that Renee had taken all of my belongings to my parents' house last night when she came because that would have just been another excuse for someone to sit and babysit me while awaiting Erin's arrival. I know the hospital staff meant no harm, but I'm honestly sick of seeing, smelling and being in this place. I placed my earbuds in and allowed K. Michelle's "Not A Little Bit" to fill my ears. Looking down for a second, I hadn't even realized there was someone standing so close to me. I damn near ran over the back of his ankles and took the back of his kneecaps out. To say I was embarrassed as hell was an understatement. Looking up, I was left speechless. This man was so sexy and instead of going off or having an evil glare on his face, he was actually laughing at me. Removing my earbuds, I began to apologize for my carelessness instantly.

"I apologize, I wasn't paying any attention. I'm so excited to get out of here."

"It's coo', Amoy. Long as you didn't hurt yourself I'm coo'," he said with the cutest smile.

"Ummm, my name is Lee, not Amoy. I'm sorry, you must have me confused with someone else, but I'm fine. I didn't hurt myself, it was your ankles and kneecaps in danger." I tried to lighten my tone because I came off a little rude when correcting him on my name. He let out a light laugh and I was glad he wasn't offended by my tone.

"Well, let me properly introduce myself. I'm Zion, and Amoy means beautiful goddess. I'm sorry if I offended you, Ms. Lee. I was just calling it how I see it."

"Oh, ok!" I said, a little embarrassed that I had tried to correct him and here he was offering me a compliment while I'm looking a hot mess. "I'm not offended. I've just never been referred to as Amoy. I guess you can say I'm a little naïve when it comes to foreign language."

"So, I take it you're from around here?" he asked as if he wasn't and I was happy for that. I didn't need for this random guy to be one of my brother's friends or even worse, Coby's friends, while he was standing here flirting with me.

"Yes, I'm from here. Columbus born and raised, how about you?" I asked, knowing good and well I would've noticed a nigga looking this good some time or another around the city. Columbus may be large as far as the size, but it's not hard to know a person without actually knowing them.

"Nah, I'm actually not from around here. I came up here to visit my grandma. I was born and raised in Atlanta, Georgia." *No wonder he had a slight accent,* I thought to myself.

"Lee, I've been texting and calling your phone to tell you I'm outside and you in here steady choppin it up like a bitch ain't been outside waiting on you." Erin came towards me talking shit and rolling her neck with a smile on her face. I looked down at my phone and sure enough, she had blew my shit down, but I didn't hear it because I had removed my earbuds when this handsome man in front of me caught my attention. Well, I should say when I almost ran over this handsome man in front of me.

"I'm sorry, Zion. It was nice talking to you and meeting you! Again, sorry about running into you!" I said as Erin positioned herself behind my wheelchair, preparing to take me to her car.

"Nah, I got it shorty, just pull your car up. I'll wheel her out." Zion surprised me and waved Erin in the direction of the door so he could push me outside instead. The kind gesture caught me off guard a little, I had to admit. Erin's ass didn't think to ask twice. Instead, she headed toward the exit and allowed this stranger to just wheel me away.

"I would like to get to know you if that's ok with you. I would've asked to take you out but I see you're a little out of commission at the moment, so I'll just ask can I call you sometimes? That is until you're up and able to actually take me up on my offer," Zion asked, causing me to blush. Thank goodness he was standing behind me or I would've been so embarrassed. Here I was sitting in the wheelchair looking a hot ass mess and he wanted to take me out so he could get to know me. Yeah, it was obvious this nigga wasn't from around here.

"Yeah, that's fine," was all I could get out before we were approaching Erin's car and she was getting out of the driver side, heading around to open the passenger door for me. Zion handed me his iPhone and of course, I took no time entering my phone number.

"Nice meeting you, Amoy. I look forward to talking to you. Aye, I hope you didn't fake me out and give me no bogus number," he said, causing not only me but Erin to laugh as well.

"No, no! Not at all. Thanks for pushing me to the car and I look forward to hearing from you again," I said while sliding into the passenger seat of Erin's car before shutting the door. Instead of turning to walk back into the hospital, he watched as Erin pulled away from the entrance of the hospital. I hadn't realized that I was cheesing until Erin spoke up.

"Ok, bitch, spill the tea. Who the hell is that fine ass nigga that got you over there showing all your damn teeth, and why the hell is he calling you another bitch name?" Erin asked, laughing hard as hell.

"Bitch, shut the hell up." I mushed her arm playfully before taking a deep breath. "Girl, some guy I ran into with my damn wheelchair not paying no damn attention to where I was going. He said Amoy means beautiful goddess in some other place or some shit. I thought the same thing when he first said it until he corrected my ass in the politest way possible. Had me looking all silly and shit for trying to check him for callin' me the wrong name." We both laughed and then my alert tone went off, notifying me that I had a new text message. When an unknown number showed across my screen with a different area code, the same silly smile I was just wearing reappeared on my face.

404-614-0929: Its Zion, lock me in, Amoy.

Me: Got it!

"Damn, you got it like that, Lee? Nigga texting you already. Shit, we ain't even hit the freeway yet. Bitch still got the juice and shit I see, with your hair looking a hot fuckin' mess!" Erin said before turning up the music and heading toward the freeway to my parents' house.

Like expected, my parents went above and beyond to ensure I came home happy. It had been a little over two months since I was discharged from the hospital and surprisingly, I was recovering faster than anyone expected. The physical therapist, nurses and even doctors were surprised by my progress. The way I looked at it, the faster I recovered and got my shit close to normal, the faster I would have them out of my hair and wouldn't have to worry about people treating me like a damn handicap. Now don't get me wrong, the special treatment was wonderful, but I can't stand depending on anyone for my every beck and call; I like having my independence. Shit, I just recently became a full adult when I moved out so to be watched or treated like a baby wasn't my cup of tea any longer. Granted, I wasn't cleared to drive just yet, but that didn't stop my parents and brother, Kris, from purchasing me a new car. I was shocked because I wasn't expecting it, but I'm extremely grateful. The 2012 cherry red Chevy Cobalt fit me perfectly.

I hadn't seen Coby, but that hasn't stopped him from calling, texting, or messaging me on Facebook, Instagram or even Twitter. Coby wasn't taking us being over for an answer. He even went as far as coming to my physical therapy sessions and sitting outside. I didn't actually see him with my own eyes but he would send text messages or pictures of me walking into the building, just to show me he was around. That shit freaked me out on a whole different level. He was really starting to take things overboard. As bad as I wanted Kris to get at this nigga, I still couldn't bring myself to tell my brother about

Coby. I'm now an adult and it's my responsibility to handle my own relationship problems without the help of my big brother. I told Renee about it and since I practically begged her not to tell anyone the first time I confided in her, she insisted that I file a restraining order against him and file harassment charges so in case he tried anything I would have a paper trail so he could be punished for his actions the next time around. Keeping it real, I was hoping I wouldn't have to experience a next time around, but at the rate he was going, I know I will have to eventually face him whether I want to or not.

Rod is still here in Columbus and he even mentioned his decision to move here for good to help his sister out within the next few months. Although Rod had been around my family and had basically become part of the family since the day of my accident, I have yet to meet any of his family. Not only did Rod's sister live here in Columbus, Ohio, but his parents as well. Up until the accident, I hadn't known that Rod had family here in Ohio. Rod had never mentioned his family so I never pressured him about them or asked about them. It's not that I wouldn't like to meet his family, it's just we have never taken the time out to plan any meet and greet type of events. Besides, Rod and I are friends, so it's not like he needed to rush to take me home and meet his momma. Rod is super cool. Over the past couple of months of us being close he has become like one of my girls, but the male version. I'm almost one hundred percent sure he doesn't feel the same because of little comments he makes whenever he's under the influence, but I try to pretend that I don't hear him or that he never mentioned it the next day when he sobers up. You know they say a drunk tongue speaks a sober heart and that's the only reason I know that Rod sees me as being more than a potential best friend. If it wasn't for the way we started, maybe I could look at him as more than a friend, but I don't ever see us crossing those lines. Rod has plenty of female friends and little thots he fucks with, but he refuses to get serious with any of them with claims of being too busy, yet his ass is always over my parents' house or with his sister. I think that's just an excuse to continue to be the baby thot that he is because he is all-around a total package for someone looking for a boyfriend.

Although I haven't been able to officially go on a date with Zion, the guy I met at the hospital a couple of months ago when I got discharged, that hadn't stopped us from getting to know each other. I didn't mind us moving at a snail's pace because I was in no way, shape or form ready to rush into another situation with all the headache and heartache my relationship with Coby caused me. Zion and I talk, text, or FaceTime all day and night. You would think we would run out of shit to talk about by now but with him, the conversations flow so easily. His personality is all-around wonderful. Even though my recovery is going really well, I still didn't want to go out on an actual date until I could drive and walk without the help of a crutch or cane. Zion comes to Columbus once a week to spend time with his grandma who has been in and out of the hospital since the day I met him, so when he's in town he stops by and visits me. Getting to know him is fun because every day I learn something new and it makes me like him even more. I can see myself really feeling Zion and making something happen between the two of us in the near future but for the moment, I'll take it day by day without any sort of rush. I'll never get too comfortable though because I thought Coby was perfect up until a year and a half after we got together. It's like I didn't learn who the real Coby was until it was too late, and I refuse to go through any crazy shit like that again.

RENEE

"I don't know what the fuck to do! I can't believe he would really do some stupid shit like this, and of all places at my job!" I screamed into the phone.

"Calm down, Nae. I already texted Erin. She's on her way to pick you up and Kris is downstairs so I'm 'bout to go fill him in. I know you didn't want to involve him but shit, enough is enough and quite frankly, I'm sick of this motherfucker and his bullshit," Lee protested. All I could do was let out a loud sigh. Lee was in fact right; enough was enough and this was the last fucking straw. My daughter rides in my car and I need my job to take care of her, so coming to my job showing his ass then turning around and fucking up my car was beyond overboard. Mark's ass sent so many idle threats I had begun to think he was just running his mouth, but him being on the block list for so long and me not taking any of his calls at work when he called must have set him over the edge. Mark showed up to my fucking job and showed his natural black ass. My supervisor and head coordinator are in the middle of a meeting at the moment, discussing the outcome of this situation. I'm sure nothing good can come from this so I'm mentally preparing myself for the shit they are going to lay on me any moment now. Standing, looking at my fucking car with all the windows busted out and dents from Mark having a field day with my car with a steel baseball bat was causing my blood to boil. As much as I wasn't a confrontational person, I'm ready to go show my ass at his momma's house because she's the one who raised such a bitch made nigga.

"Ok, Lee, my supervisor is heading my way now. I will call you after I speak with him."

"Make sure you call me and let me know what they say. I'm about to head downstairs now and fill Kris in on what the fuck just happened."

"I'll make sure to call you as soon as I finish, I promise. Please tell Kris to at least wait until I get there before he makes any decisions."

"I will, but you know how he is. Kris ain't going to hear shit I say after I tell him the story."

"You right. Ok, I gotta go."

"Ok." We ended our call right as my supervisor was calling my name to come into his office. Of all days Mark chose to show his ass, he just had to pick the day the head coordinator was in the building conducting meetings. This shit is just way too much right now.

"Ms. Johns, have a seat please," my supervisor, Mr. Allen, suggested as I walked into his office to accompany him as well as Mr. Intel, the coordinator. Having a seat across the desk from Mr. Allen and beside Mr. Intel, I couldn't control my leg from bouncing out of nervousness. I had never missed a day of work other than my scheduled off days, let alone been reprimanded for something that was out of my control.

"Ms. Johns, I would first like to say that I am completely appalled at the situation that took place at our establishment today as a result of your personal life. This is something I would have never expected, especially coming from such a great employee as yourself. Working with you over the past four years has been nothing but a great pleasure and after discussing everything with Mr. Intel, we have come to a conclusion. Although you have no control over the behaviors of your friends, this is still not a situation we can turn a blind eye to because of the amount of attention it caused and damage that was done on our property. Unfortunately, we will have to terminate you from your position. You will need to turn in your badge concluding this meeting. This is nothing against you personally or your work ethic, but simply because it is bad for business as well as unsafe for our patients to have to experience any of the drama they had to witness today. I apologize to have to inform you of this after all you encountered today, but we have to keep the company's best interest at heart." Mr. Allen continued to talk but I could no longer hear the words that were escaping his mouth; I could only see his lips moving at a rapid pace. I couldn't believe I was sitting here being fired for the stupid bullshit Mark did. Knowing I have a child to take care of, it was careless of him to ever come to my job with nonsense with the possibility that I could get in trouble for his actions. Mark was trying his hardest to ruin my life and if you ask me, he was off to a great start.

"Ms. Johns, if you could sign the paperwork that's in front of you before heading to clear your locker, please." I grabbed the black ink pen laying on the desk and signed my John Hancock. As bad as I wanted to cry, I was too in shock and pissed to allow the sadness to overtake me. After signing my signature on the last page, I cleared my voice before speaking and standing to my feet.

"I would first like to start by apologizing for everything that took place today. Had I known things would have happened the way they did today, I would have done my hardest to intervene. I appreciate the experience and opportunity I had with you both and this company. I totally understand that you have no other choice but to let me go and I can only hope to land a position with a company that is half as great as this one in the future. Again, I apologize and you gentlemen have a great day." Holding my head high, I removed my work badge and placed it on top of the paperwork I had just signed and headed out of his office to go empty my locker as instructed, before leaving the premises. I was happy they didn't have security escorting me around the building like they would have normally done if they fired a person. I had been through enough humiliating situations for the day and that would only cause me to lose it.

Walking outside, I was upset yet relieved to see my car being loaded onto the flatbed tow truck and Dupree waiting for me in his car. I'm assuming when Lee told Kris he called Dupree and they canceled Erin from coming. Dupree wore a look on his face I had only witnessed one time other than today, and I wasn't ready to face him.

Getting into the car, Dupree hadn't even allowed me to completely close my door before he started.

"Kris called and told me what the fuck happened here. I can only guess by the look on your face that you lost your job because of this lame ass dude. As mad as I want to be with you, I can't allow myself to blame you for his bitch ass actions. But let me ask you something, Nae, how long this nigga been fuckin' with you, honestly?"

"Honestly, bae, he has never stopped fucking with me but I placed him on the block list so I wouldn't be bothered by his shit. I just never thought he would take things this far. I thought he was just trying to put fear in me. I really didn't think he would do anything, especially not this, bae. I can't believe he would stoop so low," I said as tears began to escape my eyes.

"Nae, baby, I don't know why you wouldn't expect him to try some bitch shit like this after all the shit that nigga has put you through. I don't put shit past nobody, especially a nigga like Mark. Why wouldn't you tell me he continued to bother you? As your man, Renee, you have to trust me enough to let me know some shit like that and maybe none of this shit would have ever taken place. It's too late now to fix what already happened but from this moment forward, you got to keep it one hundred with a nigga. As your man, Renee, it's my job to be here to protect you and handle him, not yours."

"I'm sorry, baby. I promise not to ever keep anything else like this away from you. I just didn't feel it was worth even discussing. I didn't want Mark to cause problems or drama within our relationship with all his tactics."

"Listen, baby, can't nobody cause drama or problems between us but us. The shit outsiders do can't affect us unless we allow it to. I know I for damn sure am not about to let a nothing ass nigga like Mark tear apart what we are building. I love you, Nae, and calm down. When I tell you I got this, trust me, I got this."

"I love you too baby." As bad as I didn't want to face it, shit was about to get heated. Dupree is level headed when he is mad but Kris, on the other hand, I'm sure was thirty-eight hot and there was no reasoning with him whenever he got that pissed. Between the bullshit Mark and Coby were pulling, I didn't know who was going to get it worse. It's almost like they were in competition with who could cause the most mayhem.

After everything I went through yesterday, I woke up today determined to have a better day. I chose to leave everything behind me and move forward. Dupree is my man so I decided to trust him to handle Mark and carry on with my life and forget the worries of dealing with him. Today Dupree left me his car so that I could take care of all the shit I needed to until my car gets fixed. Thank goodness for insurance and the cameras outside of the building. I won't have to come out of pocket for any expenses, except for the five-hundred-dollar deductible. Sanai starts daycare today for the first time and although I'm nervous, I'm also anxious for my baby to begin school. I waited until she turned one before enrolling her into any daycare programs because my parents were totally against it. After a great deal of debate on her social skills and education, they finally gave in and agreed with me about putting her into a daycare program. With Sanai being in school during the day it allows me to look for another job and take care of everything else during my free hours.

Sanai surprisingly adapted well. She didn't cry or even try to leave with me. Instead, she ran over and started to engage herself with the other little kids as if she had been knowing them all along. I was happy she didn't protest staying without me because it would have made it even harder for me to leave her there alone. No sooner than I opened the door to leave the facility, in came Dame's baby mom, Kena, and their son. Of course, she had to be petty and make sure I knew it was her by screaming Lil Dame's name as if I didn't already know who the fuck she was. I be damned if she hadn't dropped him off and ran right the fuck back out of the building before I could even get in my car and pull off. The same friend she was at the club with was sitting on the passenger side looking in her direction, ready to be petty right along with her.

"Kena, Dame calling you. He's probably at the house waiting on your ass to get back."

"Answer and tell him I'm on the way there to pop this pussy for a real nigga!" she yelled back, giggling.

"The phone stopped ringing already. Shit, I need to call back and see if he got that nigga Dupree with him. God knows that man can get it again." The friend was being real extra and they both found that shit hilarious, unlike me. If it wasn't for the fact that we were at the daycare I probably would've called Erin up there and saw how the fuck Kena reacted, but now wasn't the time and this wasn't the place. I simply shook my head at the two Petty Bettys, got in my car and pulled off in the direction of the grocery store.

I only planned on stopping by the grocery store to pick up a few items since we already had food in the house, but certain shit we tend to run out of a lot quicker than others, such as juice and fruit. Approaching the checkout counter, I'll be damn if the person right in front of me, loading their cart onto the belt wasn't Mark's new girl-friend, Nyla. I'm hoping like hell Mark isn't in the damn store with her or outside waiting for her to complete her shopping. Today must be run into the side bitch day or something because I don' ran into three of these bitches within the last damn hour. Nyla and I had never had any previous issues, but we weren't friends either so I planned on pretending as if I didn't see her. Just as soon as I thought I was in the clear, Nyla turned around and faced me. I was caught off guard by her round baby bump that I hadn't noticed when she was facing the oppo-site direction. I knew at Sanai's birthday party she had a little pudge but I assumed that it was just fat, not that she was actually with child. I'm almost certain it's Mark's baby because they are currently still together and from what I last heard, doing well.

"Hey, Renee, I didn't expect to ever run into you here. Instead of beating around the bush I'm just going to address the issue now since we are face to face. Why is it you feel like you should keep Sanai away from her father because of yawl issues? I tried to stay out of it but since my son will be here within the next few months, I wanted to know if it was going to be a problem for Sanai to be around her broth-er." I shifted my head to the side and gave her the look of confusion mixed with anger. Like did this bitch really think she had just confronted me about my child with the wrong information? I let out a smirk before responding to the ditzy bitch.

"Look, Nyla, I don't know what the fuck Mark is over there filling your head with but the information you have is all wrong, so I'm just going to say this and leave it at that. Sanai will not be around your, or should I say y'alls son. Oh, and by the way, you should have stayed out of it because it has nothing to do with you. I would appreciate it if you grabbed your groceries and continued on with your day as if you didn't just see me, please and thanks in advance." With the last comment, I started grabbing the few items I had and placing them on the belt so the cashier could begin to ring my items up since she was now finished with Nyla. The look on Nyla's face was of pure embarrassment, but I don't give a fuck. If you're going to speak on something, make sure you know what the hell you're talking about before trying to approach someone about something you know nothing about. I can't wait to get out of this store and call Lee about the fuckery I've experienced today between the Three Musketeers.

While putting the groceries away, I decided to call Lee and put her up on what happened today. Of course, Lee was ready to call Erin and Netia up to go smack them hoes into their place. She wasn't even fully healed yet but was still ready to throw them hands up. I had to laugh at how much of a little firecracker my younger sister was, no matter her situation. I still had a few more hours before picking Sanai up from school and Dupree would be working overtime today. Since the business he and Dame just recently started is still in its beginning stages it requires a lot of his attention. They had come up with a car detailing shop that also offered the basic work and repair options if needed. Dupree was giving more than a hundred and ten percent of his effort to get things on the right track for success and I couldn't be more proud of him. His time lately was stretched between not only working full time in construction with his pops but full time at his very own business as well. I didn't mind because since finding out that Sanai was in fact his daughter, Dupree had been hustling less and less and more devoted to working his construction job and business. The goal was for him to be completely done with all the slanging shit within six months of his business opening. We were only in the first month but I could see him putting a great deal of effort to reach his deadline successfully.

I feel it all over my body (I feel it all over my body)
I dream about you when I sleep (yes)

Hearing Dupree's ringtone "*You're The One*" by Dondria going off took me completely out of my zone in the kitchen. I was only wiping down the counters and cabinets since there wasn't anything else needing to be cleaned around the house. "Hey, baby," I said sweetly into the phone, greeting my man.

"Sup baby, what you doing?"

"Nothing, cleaning the kitchen. How's your day going?"

"Oh ok, make sure you get some rest while you're free, babe. The house is already cleaned if you haven't noticed. My day is going good, thanks for asking. How's your day going, baby?"

"My day has been very comical, but no complaints. I know it's clean but after I put away the groceries I just went and grabbed, I wiped the counters and cabinets down if you don't mind," I replied jokingly.

"Nah, I don't mind baby. I just don't want you up doing shit all day. Take this time off of work as your break, baby. You were due for a break. You've been going hard, working and being a mother; you needed some you time, baby. I got a surprise for you too, by the way."

"I'm fine, baby. I'm not tired, I'm actually well rested. Ohhhhh, baby, I love surprises. I can't wait to see what you got up your sleeve this time."

"I know you do love surprises, with your spoiled ass."

"What did I do to deserve you?" I asked Dupree, but not really looking for a response. Dupree is such a wonderful companion, friend, lover, father and person. Although I wasted a lot of time pushing him away, I'm glad I finally opened my eyes before I missed out on having the chance to be with such a great man.

"I don't know what you did but whatever it was, I'm glad you got me because I couldn't ask for a better woman. I'm about to get back to work, I'll see you later, baby. I love you, Nae baby."

"Love you too baby." Ending the call with Dupree, I couldn't help but smile and admire that man. I decided against telling Dupree the details of the shenanigans I faced today because if you asked me, it wasn't worth it. One thing I didn't have to worry about was my man cheating on me. Dupree worked too hard to prove to me he was the man I needed to go and sneak around with a rat ass female that played the yes man to another nothing ass bitch. Now, I do plan on informing him about the conversation I had with Nyla, only for the simple fact that it involves Mark and I promised Dupree I wouldn't keep any more secrets when it came to the Mark situation.

Since tonight would be a late night for Dupree I chose to make taco salad so that it would still be a filling and tasty meal once reheated, depending on the time he got home. I'm excited to see how Sanai's first day at school went. They didn't call me and I did a damn good job by not calling up there checking on her. When I walked into the building, I could hear my baby laughing. There's something about being a mother; you can detect your child's cries, laughter and voice out of a million and one other kid, no matter how loud or quiet it may be. Sanai's teacher told me that Sanai had a great day and transitioned very well for this to be her first day and the first time in a setting around such a large number of kids. She also bragged to me about how smart Sanai is for her age. Knowing that my baby enjoyed school made me feel even better about making the choice to enroll her. I know she enjoys being with her grandparents but it's time for her to be around some kids her age instead of adults twenty-four seven. Sanai is already grown for her age. I don't want her to have poor social skills with children around her age because of being up under us adults all the time. Walking outside of the daycare, I almost screamed at the sight before me. Dupree was parked next to his Charger with a gold 2013 Chevy Malibu with a huge red bow on top of it. My car was only supposed to be in the shop being fixed; I wasn't expecting him to purchase me a brand new car. Dupree got out the car and headed in my direction, reaching his arms out for Sanai and I. Just as we reached Dupree, Kena's messy ass was pulling into the parking lot with her sidekick in the passenger seat. The looks on their faces were priceless. I'm sure they were pissed and wouldn't be wasting any time making their smart comments this time around. Dupree wasted no time wrapping one of his arms around me and kissing my lips, all while removing Sanai from me with his other arm.

"Aww, thanks, baby. I can't believe you got me a new car. What happened to my old one?"

"You're welcome baby! You deserve it and I just went ahead and left it alone. There was no need to fix it if you have a new one. We are starting fresh! Now if you still want it I have it up at my shop. If not, I'll just go ahead and use it as a display once we put some work into it."

"Hell no I don't want it! I'm happy with this car, baby! You sure can keep that car. Where my keys anyway?" I asked, while walking towards my new vehicle.

"They are still in the ignition . Do you want Sanai to ride home with me or you want her to ride in mommy's new car too?" Dupree asked with a grin on his face matching mine.

"She can ride with you so we don't have to switch her car seat over. Plus, we're going to the same place anyhow." I couldn't help the grin that was plastered on my face. Hopping in my new car, I placed my seat belt on and waited for Dupree to fasten our daughter into her car seat in his car. Once he made sure Sanai was secure in her seat and prepared to pull off, I placed my gear in drive and headed in the direction of my home. Driving home, my mind began to wander while figuring out all the new gadgets and tricks to my new vehicle. This is the happiest I've been in quite some time. I can't believe Dupree and I are doing so well. I can literally say for once that I have no complaints about my life right about now. I don't have to worry about my man creeping or cheating on me, let alone worry about my man going upside my head for his own shortcomings. My daughter is doing well, my sister is recovering at a speedy rate, my parents are ok and I'm happy. What more can I ask for?

Shit has actually been too good to be true. Outside of Lee's accident a few months back, everything has been smooth sailing. Dame and I have been doing good, thank God. Other than the fact he has Petty Betty for a baby mom, we are good. As long as the bitch never touches my car again and keeps that mouth close when I'm around, I won't touch her, but the moment she steps out of line again I'm tagging that ass. Dame knows I'm ready to beat the breaks off of her just on the strength of her mouth always being so slick, so he keeps us far apart. I find it funny because Dame is so quick to turn up on somebody but tries to be the peacemaker all of a sudden between the two of us. Lil Dame hasn't been around me as much and I'm sure it has something to do with the fact that Dame and I are always together, which Kena hates oh so much. Since Kena's sorry ass wants to play games and hold Lil Dame over Dame's head, he has met with an attorney recently to go to court for visitation rights or even joint custody if everything works in his favor. Once he goes through the courts there won't be much she can do to protest what the judge orders. I hope she's having fun using their son as a pawn for now because all that shit is about to come to a halt. Eventually, she's just going to have to accept the fact that her son will be around me whether she likes it or not. Shit, it's not as if he doesn't want to be around me. Lil Dame actually loves me. Shit, I think he likes being with me and his dad more than being with her ratchet ass. I thought that he would be timid or maybe even shy around me but that little boy acts like I'm his momma when he is around.

Dame and I have been talking lately about me moving into his house with him and letting go of my apartment since we are always together anyhow. I really don't have a problem with me moving into his place; it's a very nice three-bedroom condo on the Eastside. I just don't want to lose my independence by moving with him. Niggas tend to change up when they feel you need them or depend on them for anything. Dame doesn't seem like the type to throw up what he has done for me in my face or change shit up once I'm living under his roof instead of my own, but you never know. In my case, I don't want to find out once it's too late. Then again, the only way to know how he will react is actually experiencing it. It will be a different experience for both of us once we actually live together in one house and have Lil Dame. Even though it will be a big change, I'm ready to take on whatever this relationship has to bring.

"Erin, can you bring me a towel in here? I forgot my shit and it's cold as fuck!" Dame yelled from the bathroom.

"Yeah, babe, here I come." I grabbed Dame's towel and headed toward the bathroom, but what he didn't know was he wasn't about to get out just yet.

"Babe, what you doing?" Dame asked me with a confused, yet devious smile. I walked into the bathroom ass naked, ready to get in a quick morning sex session before we both had to head our separate ways for the day.

"What? What you talking about babe?" I questioned Dame back as if I didn't know what he was talking about. Sliding the shower curtain back even further so I could join him in the shower, I caught him completely off guard as expected. Instead of climbing into the shower to wash up along with him, I climbed in and turned to face Dame and dropped to my knees. Sitting eye level with his thick, juicy dick in my face, I couldn't help but lick my lips at the sight before me. No matter how often I tasted Dame, it was never enough. It's like I craved to taste my man's dick in my mouth at least twice a day. After coating my lips with my own saliva, I grabbed Dame's thick, light skin meat with my left hand and inserted him into my warm mouth. The mixture of the hot water from the shower pouring down on me and Dame's strong grip on the back of my head caused me to zone out and go full throttle on his dick. The suction from my jaws and rapid motions of my hands were taking him to a new world and I could tell by the moans he was allowing to escape his lips. Just knowing how damn good I was sucking that dick caused my pussy to drip. If it wasn't for us being in the shower, I was sure there would be a puddle underneath where I was squatting down at. The closer Dame got to his climax, the hornier I became, but I wanted him to at least get one nut in before we had sex. Right then, I felt his dick begin to pulsate inside of my mouth and his grip became even tighter on the back of my head. Dame started fucking my face back and his legs were jerking as his dick jumped in the back of my throat. I knew right then that at any moment, he was about to let loose. The feeling of Dame's nut rushing to the back of my throat caused me to suck a little harder, attempting to empty him out. As soon as I felt he was done, I swallowed and started sucking again to get that dick right back up where I needed it. When I felt his dick coming back to life, I stood up and turned my back towards Dame and reached down to grab my ankles for support. Dame slapped his hard, thick head against my ass cheeks and then began to slide it up and down the creases, making the desire to feel him inside of me grow even stronger. When Dame spread my ass cheeks apart, the anticipation grew even more, causing me to scoot back toward him to help speed up the process. When I felt the thick tip of his dick spreading the opening of my pussy, I wanted to cream right then and there, but I had to hold out a little while longer. "Damn babe, that pussy ready for daddy! You better hold them ankles and don't let go," Dame seductively told me in the sexiest raspy tone I had ever heard in my life. I closed my eyes and prepared for the dick lashing I was about to receive. As Dame pumped inside of me, I slowly threw it back at him, matching his rhythm. The sounds of our wet skin hitting and the mixture of my juices splashing with the water was mind blowing.

"I'm 'bout to cum, daddy, shit! Don't stop. Right there, daddy. Right thereeee." I felt Dame hitting my G-spot and I wanted him to punish my shit to the point where I couldn't help but explode right then and there. The tingling sensation that felt like an urge to pee was approaching and before I knew it, I was squirting all over. My cum not only trickled down the inside of my thighs, but Dame's as well.

"Damn, girl, that shit feels amazing. Don't worry, baby, daddy 'bout to bust all in this good shit. Keep throwing that fat ass back just like that. Ummmm, yeah, just like that." Dame didn't have to instruct me on how to please him, but just doing so was arousing. Dame grunted as he was spilling all of his semen inside of me with the death grip on my ass cheeks.

....

I can't and won't complain. At the moment, shit seems to be going my way without any complaints. I'm sure Kena's messy ass is somewhere in the cut ready to pop up with some bullshit, but that's cool too because I'm ready to pop that bitch smack dead in her shit anyhow. Even though she hadn't directly come at me, I've read all her subliminal messages and post over social media she shoots towards me. On top of her slick comments here and there, Renee happens to run into this messy hoe on a daily basis and she forever has something to say when Renee is around. I don't know when that hoe is going to get enough of trying to be sneaky and fuck up what Dame and I have. Shit, although we haven't been official for a year yet, we are approaching the year point for us fucking around so at this point, she should have gotten the fucking point by now. But I guess some bitches will never learn no matter what the fuck you say or do to them. I don't know if it's the fact that I'm a younger bitch that bothers her or the fact that Dame just ain't stunting her ass. To think that the nasty bitch has herpes and still wants to fuck around with a clean dick just speaks on how low she is. Shit, not just any clean dick, but *my* clean dick, and it ain't going nowhere. Well, at least no time soon. Just as I got ready to clock out of work I got a call from my mom, which in my opinion was rare because ever since the day I moved out, our relationship has been more of a strain than a pleasure. It's not like I dislike her or anything but we definitely don't see eye to eye. It's like she's living her life and I'm living mine, but that's cool with me. When she called I could tell by the tone of her voice there was something she felt the need to tell me. The only thing I was hoping is that it wasn't some fucked up news to rain on my parade I had been enjoying as of late. When she told me that my sorry ass long lost sperm donor had appeared at her door and was looking for me, I was in complete shock. All those years I wondered where that punk ass nigga went, carrying on as if he never gave a fuck about me, and now all of a sudden he finally decided to resurface once I was grown, on my own and no longer gave two fucks. I agreed to allow my mom to pass my number along to the scum ass nigga. I just hoped that I wouldn't regret allowing him to make contact with me after all these years. The last time I remember ever seeing or even talking to my sperm donor I was about five or six and he dropped off some school clothes, then got into a huge argument with my mom; he never showed his face around us again after that day. The nigga didn't even come around when I graduated from high school two years ago, so as far as I knew, he had fallen off the face of the earth or was at least six feet under somewhere. You would think since I was his only known child that he would care a little more, but I guess that meant nothing to him. As far as I was concerned his family wasn't about shit either. Well, it's not like they lived here in Columbus anyways. They lived somewhere down south from what I remember my mom telling me when I was younger when I would ask to go visit his side of the family.

When my sperm donor called my phone I was a little shocked that he was requesting to meet up with me so soon on such short notice. Not only was he determined to meet up with me today, he wanted it to be a formal type of dinner with other relatives. He told me he would explain and introduce me to them upon us meeting up at dinner. As bad as I wanted to decline, I took the sorry ass nigga up on his offer. I sent Dame a text message informing him on what happened today and he felt it was a great idea. I believe Dame was all for it based on the fact that he lost one of his parents at a young age so he felt that it was a blessing to have both parents here, living and able to actually sit down and talk to them. In my opinion, my dad was basically a complete stranger so I didn't want to go to this dinner alone. I wanted Dame to go along with me because for real, I'm kind of nervous about meeting up with this man and his family after so many years, but Dame felt it was best if I go alone this time. Dame promised he would accompany me the next go round. Eric, also known as my long lost father, sent me a text with the address of the restaurant we would be meeting at this evening. When I googled the address and found out we were meeting up at Eddie Merlot's in Polaris, I was a little in shock. I was expecting more of a Red Lobster or Cheesecake Factory type of dinner, but wherever he chooses was fine with me. Shit, the least he could do was treat me to a nice dinner after all these years of not doing a damn thing for me.

Walking into the restaurant, I was very pleased with the big, beautiful paintings on the walls and the seating arrangements. This place was for sure something I was going to have to put Dame up on for an anniversary or date night. My poor baby was so hood rich mentally he felt like anything that didn't have a drive-through was a good dinner date, which I would have to disagree with. The hostess greeted me and I gave her the name Eric. After informing her of my party, she led me in the direction of those awaiting my arrival. I made sure to arrive about twenty minutes late so that I would be the last guest to be seated. Shit, if he was trying to please me he had to be on my time. Plus, I was so indecisive on what to wear that it took longer than I expected to get dressed. As soon as we reached the table I was in shock to only see a table seating five people; I was expecting more for some odd reason. Of the four people seated at the table, one being my father, there was some older lady I assumed was his woman, a younger guy that resembled my father very much so, and the bitch Ciara that is Kena's sidekick. I'll be damned if the empty chair left for me wasn't sitting right across from the enemy. I couldn't help but wonder to myself what the fuck she was doing here and her connection to my father.

"Hello, Erin! How are you, baby girl? You look amazing. Still as beautiful as you were the last time I saw you," Eric greeted me, snapping me out of my death stare and trance I had fixed on Ciara.

"Umm, hey, thank you. I'm doing well, how about yourself?" I returned the friendly greeting as I pulled out my chair to be seated at the same time he was standing to embrace me for a hug and attempted to pull my chair out. I didn't want to appear too standoffish or rude, so I allowed him to embrace me. I can't lie and say that all of this didn't feel a bit awkward, but I was ready to see what this man had to say, so I continued to play along with his caring act.

"Hello, Erin, it's a pleasure to finally meet you," the lady sitting next to Eric stood up, greeting me with the biggest smile on her face as if she had come in contact with her long-lost daughter as well.

"Hi!" was all I could muster up to say because although I assumed this was Eric's woman, I still had no idea who this bitch was.

"I'm sorry. Excuse my manners, Erin. This is my wife, Anita. Anita, as you already know this is my baby girl, Erin." I snickered because I found it funny how he referred to me as his baby girl as if he really gave a fuck about me.

"Erin, this is your younger brother, Eric Jr. and your older sister, Ciara." I'm sure my face expressed how I felt because Anita coughed a little and broke the silence. I'll be damn if this bitch ain't my muthafucking sister. I couldn't even greet that bitch because as far as I was concerned, I still owed that bitch an ass whooping. I couldn't wait for the dinner to be over so I could inform the girls about what the fuck I discovered today. I knew this dinner shit was too good to be true and some fuckery was going to come out of it.

As dinner went on I learned my younger brother is cool as fuck. Although he is only two years younger than me, he is very mature for the age of eighteen. EJ, as they called him, is also a fucking clown; he always had some slick shit to say on the low. Over the conversations during dinner, I discovered all of my father's children had different mothers and Anita mothered not one of us. I wondered how the fuck she could marry a scum bag that had three kids out here in the world and had only been a part of one of their lives, and that was Eric Jr. The only reason he was probably part of Eric Jr.'s life was because his mother had died at birth, leaving my father no other choice but to either man up by raising him as a single parent or ship his one and only son off to Child Services. My father also mentioned the fact that he had just recently reconnected with Ciara as well, but from the way she acted you would have thought that nigga had been around her entire life. Ciara was brown nosing the fuck out of my dad and playing the daddy's girl role well. I don't know if she did it to get under my skin or had she really felt that close to his sorry ass. Ciara not being from Ohio all made sense now. My father was able to run and skip from state to state because he had bitches back in his home state, as well as here in Ohio.

Dinner went better than I expected, considering Ciara and I barely said a word to each other. She couldn't even really make eye contact with me. *Ol' scary ass bitch,* I thought to myself. It's funny that I hadn't realized until now that me and this skank had so many facial similarities. This whole situation is mind blowing. When dinner was over, I was actually happy that I came and got the chance to meet with not only my father, but also my siblings I knew nothing about. My father told me that he reached out to my mother several times but she refused to have anything to do with him or his life because of him up and leaving us instead of manning up and taking care of his responsibilities like he promised her he would. I could believe that too because my mom is one bitter ass bitch and once you do one wrong to her she will never allow you to live that shit down. My mom is like the energizer bunny that keeps going and going. Shit, she still threw up little shit I said or did when I was younger that pissed her off. At the closing of dinner, I promised my father I would be sure to contact him as well as meet back up with him before he left Columbus and returned back home. EJ and I exchanged numbers during dinner when he texted me talking about our sister on the low. I'm sure the bitch felt uncomfortable because of the bond we had created so soon, but neither of us really gave two fucks how she was feeling.

It had been a few weeks since I met up with my other "family" and so far it seems to be a good move. My father reached out to me on a daily basis now, even if it was only to say hello and see how my day was going. EJ and I, on the other hand, talked like we had known each other our entire lives; we were so much alike it was sickening. He was just a male version of me. Ciara was a different story; I hadn't heard anything about her. I just knew for a fact the bitch would resurface with some sort of drama with Kena just on the strength that she knew I would attempt to respect my father by not going upside her head. Little did she know, she had earned an ass whooping prior to me discovering we were related, so she would still get it when the time was right. As far as I was concerned, she was no kin to me other than the fact we shared the same father. Lee, Netia, and Renee were more of my sisters than Ciara and they are all I needed. If I didn't know any better, I would think my mom was also trying to keep in contact with me more than ever now as well. I don't know if it was her guilty conscious over the fact that my father had been trying to get in contact with me and I now knew it or the fact that she had just hit me with some unpleasant news about her ongoing test to find out if she had breast cancer. Like they always say, when shits sweet, something sour has to come along. I pray that she isn't diagnosed with cancer but I always had the theory that those who have cancer either do or have done some foul shit in their life that is eating them from within. My mother is no saint so I'm sure she has some skeletons in her closet that are waiting to spill out.

"Babe, what the hell is taking you so long?" Dame yelled into the bathroom as I put the finishing touches on myself. Today was the day Dame and Dupree would be hosting their first celebration party for the signing of a big contract they recently signed at their company.

"I'm coming, dang nigga! You would rather me take my time than rush out of here looking a hot ass mess on your arm, now wouldn't you?" I questioned as if I didn't know the answer to my own question.

"Shit, I really don't give a fuck what you look like as long as you bring your ass on," Dame said and I couldn't do shit but laugh because we all knew that was a damn lie.

"Yeah, ok nigga, if you say so. Grab my phone, babe, here I come," I said, as I turned the bathroom light off and headed down the stairs to meet him in the living room.

"Damn, baby! I see why you took so long. You looking good enough to eat right now. If we don't hurry up and leave we won't be leaving period. The way I'm feeling, I'm ready to turn your ass right the fuck back around and eat that booty like some groceries. Them hips looking better than Nicki's in that dress, babe. What you trying to do, distract a nigga the entire night?" Dame said, eyeing me with his sexy ass lustful eyes. He was joking but shit, I was thinking the same thing when I laid eyes on him. It was rare for Dame to dress casual and seeing him in a button up alone had my panties dripping wet, ready to bust it wide open for my nigga.

"Well thanks, baby, you don't look too bad your damn self," I said as I bit the side of my bottom lip. I'm sure we wouldn't make it the entire night without trying to get something poppin' while at this event; that would be damn near impossible. Dame and I together are like two animals in heat around each other.

When we got to Club XO, I wasn't surprised to see our whole entire team looking like we should've been walking out on somebody's red carpet. The VIP area was shut the fuck down and there were sparklers coming, and bottles popping by the minute. When the DJ played the throwback from a few years back, "No New Friends" by Drake featuring Rick Ross and Lil Wayne, not only did our section start going nuts, but the hoes on the crowded dance floor did as well. I be damn if Dame didn't come behind me and bend my ass over so I could twerk all this ass for a real nigga. Soon as I lifted my head back up I made eye contact with Kena's weak ass standing on the dance floor, eyeing us with looks that could kill, right along with Ciara's weak ass. It's hard to believe that weak hoe and I shared the same fucking bloodline. My focus on them was broken when I saw EJ walking towards our section. My brother wasn't old enough to be in here partying with us, but shit neither was I; that didn't stop the pull my man had around the city, though.

Shit, the night was only half way over and I was lit beyond what I ever expected. The only pussy Dame would be getting tonight was some Grade A certified drunk pussy. Everyone was in over their heads, except Renee. She's the only one who seemed to be level headed with the amount of drinks being taken back. Kena hadn't made her presence known other than her little stare down and I was hoping she kept it like that because I didn't dress this cute to have to fuck a bitch up. But if need be, I will without hesitation. Rich Gang's "Tap out" filled the speakers and Dame came from behind and grabbed me by the waist and started rapping the lyrics in my ear.

> *If you hating, you just need some pussy. (Rich)*
> *She fucked up when she gave me some pussy.*
> *Say "I fuck you better than that other nigga".*
> *She say Tune "I'm 'bout to cum," I say, "I'm cumming with ya."*
> *And she don't like them pretty niggas s'ditty niggas*
> *She ride this disk her titties jiggle*
> *That's my pillows*

Dame's tone alone was enough to make me push him down on one of these couches and ride the fuck out of him right here in the VIP section for the entire club to see. Luckily, I have more class than that because that shit would be some mind blowing sex just from the excitement of everyone watching daddy put it on me. "Damn, baby, you going to make daddy take you up outta here and fuck that ass right in the parking lot, bouncing like that on a nigga dick," Dame slurred into my ear. Little did he know, I was already thinking of a plan to get some of that before we got home if I didn't pass the fuck out from being too drunk first. There was no way in hell I was going to make it the entire ride home awake and without fucking. My pussy had been calling his name since before we left the house earlier.

"Come on, daddy, let's go. I'm ready to leave anyways." As soon as those words left my lips, Dame didn't think twice about what I said. Instead, he gripped my hand and pulled me in the direction of the exit. I waved bye to my girls and he gave his niggas the head nod. They knew what we had in mind just from the urgency in our steps. Of course, we couldn't make it out of the club without the bitch, Kena, letting it be known she was in here as well. It would've been too much like right for her just to keep it moving like we weren't here and go on with her night.

"Damn, baby daddy, you're really going to walk out of this bitch like you don't see me or some shit. I know you got your little bitch with you but you could have at least greeted a bitch." Before I could correct the weak hoe, Dame was all over it.

"Look, Kena, I don't give a fuck what you talking about. Move the fuck out my way so I can go eat my girl's pussy from the back on the hood of my car before the crowd comes out. Oh, and make that your last time disrespecting her, I'm not going to tell you again." Kena's mouth dropped and she was left standing there speechless, as we headed to the car. I didn't know if those were Dame's real intentions, but I was more than ready to find out.

Renee's ass thinks she's slick. She's been buying pads and shit like she's having a period and I know for damn sure she hasn't. When you're with a person and in sync with their every move, you notice everything about them. You even begin to peep the small shit as well. I don't know if she's scared to admit it, but her pussy told on her already. It's not that Renee didn't have some fire ass pussy already, but pregnant pussy is different and I can definitely tell the difference. Although I told her that shit felt different, she blamed it on us fucking in the shower more often now. I can't say that I'm ready to have another baby, but I would never want Nae to kill my seed either. Shit, I was man enough to let my load off inside of her so I'm man enough to raise my child. This would also be a new experience for me since I wasn't able to be around for her first pregnancy with Sanai like a father is supposed to because the secret wasn't out about Sanai being mine at the time. I don't know how much longer I can pretend to not know baby girl is carrying my seed. It's only been two months since her last period, but I feel like we should be going through this together. I never want her to feel like she is in any situation alone when I'm right here by her side. Renee is really my everything and I still can't believe that we have our very own little family while looking for our first home to buy together.

"Well, hello stranger," I heard a familiar voice greet me as I looked up and made eye contact with Alisha. I was surprised to have run into her at the mall while out shopping. I only planned to run into the mall and grab a few pairs of basketball shorts from Footlocker but ended up in Saks as well as Pandora to grab Renee a just because gift.

"What's up, Alisha?" I really didn't know what else to say to her because the last time we spoke or had any form of communication I told her about Renee. When I told her about Renee and our daughter, Alisha low key spazzed out on a nigga and told me that the baby she was carrying basically wasn't mine. After that conversation, I didn't feel the need to keep in contact with her because she was no longer my woman or side thang.

"How you been? Long time no see or talk since you been with your baby's mother. I didn't expect you to completely lose contact with me once yawl got things situated between yawl two, but I guess that's how things go, huh?" Alisha said with a hint of disappointment in her voice. I never meant to string Alisha along or hurt her feelings, but my love for Renee wouldn't allow me to turn down Renee to see if what I had started with Alisha would be worth what I desired to have with Renee.

"I've been good, how about yourself?" I chose not to respond to the other part of her statement in fear of saying some shit that might hurt her even worse. The truth was now that I was with Renee, I had no need for any other females. Renee filled all my wants and desires within one woman. My woman could cook, clean, fuck and suck a nigga good; there was no reason to have friends or bitches on the side. I fought too long to have Renee and now that I have her, I'm not willing to risk losing her for some bullshit. Looking at Alisha though I couldn't deny the pregnancy glow looked good on her. Although she had to have been close to six or seven months, she still wasn't showing very much in the stomach area. Now, I can't say the same about her hips and ass; those muthafuckas had spread on a whole different level. I had to remind myself I was a taken man and to keep my eyes and mind away from that direction of her body.

"I'm doing well, aside from all this morning sickness bull crap. I'll be glad when it's all over and done with. Not to mention the fact that I crave the nastiest combinations at the weirdest times, but other than that I've been good, thanks for asking." I don't know if she threw the facts of her pregnancy in my face to see where my head was at or to get a reaction out of me but either way, I had no intention of addressing that situation until the baby came out. Until Alisha proved the child was mine, anything about the baby wasn't any of my concern. She brought all that on herself when she said the slick shit she did.

"Oh ok, well, let me get going. I have to meet up with my brother in a few and I still need to grab a few more things before I head out of here."

"Oh, I'm sorry! My fault, I didn't mean to hold you up. Go ahead and finish up your shopping. Don't be a stranger, Dupree. I miss our conversations more than anything. You were always a good friend, aside from everything else. Take care, hun," Alisha said before turning to walk away with a little pep in her step, showing off that fat ass of hers and nice sway of her hips. As bad as I wanted to deny it, a part of me wanted to get inside of that once more before deciding I would never hit her up again. The other part of me was ok with being the family man I needed and wanted to be right now. Either way, I couldn't allow my man downstairs to do all the thinking for me. I have to have some sort of self-control and now is the test of time.

The entire ride to meet up with Dame I couldn't get Alisha out of my head and it didn't help that Renee hadn't been answering her damn phone. It's not like she was busy at work or anything. She still hadn't found a new job after losing her last one. Not that I was in any type of rush because I loved waking up to breakfast before work and seeing her beautiful face before I left home each and every day. It's like Alisha was reading my mind because as I was merging off the freeway, heading over to my pops' house, my alert tone went off on my phone, notifying me of a new text message. Alisha's number was no longer saved in my phone but I recognized her phone number.

614-419-2011: Hey it was nice seeing you today. I hope you don't remain a stranger.

ME: It was good seeing you too, take care.

614-419-2011: I will and you too hun.

Instead of texting her back, I decided to just place my phone back in the cup holder and try to place her in the back of my mind where she needed to be. Pulling into my pops' driveway, I wasn't expecting to see Dame outside talking to his drama-filled ass baby mom. I swear I got tired of this bitch and she wasn't even my headache to worry about. It seemed like she just couldn't get it through her thick ass skull for some reason. I knew there was no way in hell my pops could be home because he can't stand Kena's ass and he wasn't secretive about how he felt about anything. My old man has no filter, but the shit be hilarious.

"What's up, Dee?" Dame dapped me up as I walked up on him.

"What's good, nigga?" I greeted him in return.

"Hey, Dupree, since you act like you ain't see me standing here." Kena just had to say something. I had no intentions of speaking and it really didn't matter if she spoke to me first or not.

"I ain't obligated to speak to you. The fuck? This ain't your spot. Dame, holla at me when you get done chopping it up with her, I'm 'bout to go chill inside for a second," I said over my shoulder as I walked away and let them two continue the conversation they were having prior to my arrival. I could hear Kena talking shit to Dame about my comment as I closed the screen door behind me. I don't know what Dame ever saw in her weak ass to begin with. In my opinion, she was a certified rat from the sewer, but what did my opinion matter, she wasn't the woman I had to deal with for the next eighteen years. My phone started ringing and I was hoping it wouldn't be Alisha's ass calling me back; I was glad to see Renee's name pop across the screen.

"What's up, baby, what you doing?" I said eagerly into the phone, happy to hear from my baby.

"Hey, babe. Nothing, 'bout to pick Sanai up from my parents. I left my phone on silent earlier on accident when I was taking a nap but I called you to tell you... I'm pregnant, babe, and I'm scared." Renee started crying before she could even finish her sentence. I was happy that she finally admitted to me that she was pregnant because I had already begun to assume she was. A smile crept across my face just from the thought of us bringing another child into this world. If I wasn't sure before, I knew now we were making the right decision to be looking for a new home to raise our little family in.

"Calm down, baby. Why are you crying? Sanai is good and the new baby will be too." I tried to reassure her that there was nothing for her to worry about.

"Because babe. I'm just not sure we are ready for two kids. I'm already worn out with Sanai alone, so adding another child to the equation would be a lot. I'm not working as of right now and I don't want to put the load all on you financially. I know we have help as far as a support system, but I don't want our parents raising our children just so we can make ends meet. I'm scared, babe, I'm just scared."

"Listen, baby, there is nothing to be scared about. I'm here now and I will be here then. It doesn't matter if you work or not. I'm always going to provide for you and my kids, baby. That's what a man is supposed to do. Even when I leave this earth, I'm going to make sure yawl good. Trust me when I say that I got y'all. I don't give a damn if you were to ever work another day in your life. Shit, I actually like waking up to your stankin' ass breath in the morning. Our parents don't have to raise our kids cause that's what we are going to do. TOGETHER! Stop crying, baby. I'm about to leave my pops, I'll meet you at home."

"Ok, babe, I love you. I'll see you in a few," Renee said in between sniffles.

"I love you too, Nae, and calm down before you start stressing my baby."

Instead of sticking around and waiting to talk to Dame about some business shit that could honestly wait until tomorrow, I hopped up to go home and meet my woman; my family comes first. That's where these niggas lack these days, putting everything before what matters most. My woman and our children are the most important things to me after God and if I need to go reassure my woman that everything is going to be ok, then that's exactly what the fuck I'm about to go do. Grabbing Renee, a just because gift came right on time because I'm sure she could use it right about now to pick up her spirits.

"Alright, brah, I'm 'bout to run home, Nae needs to talk to me about something. I'mma get up with you tomorrow," I told Dame as I headed towards the direction of my car. This silly ass dude was still outside entertaining Kena's ass; for what, I don't know. He better hope Erin's crazy ass don't pop up over here or all hell is going to break loose and won't nobody be here to help stop or break the shit up.

"Alright, Dee, be safe nigga," Dame said before turning and giving his attention back to Kena.

I know everybody looking at me like I'm some silly nigga, thinking I'm about to fuck around with this sick bitch. Nah, truth is, I'm not going to fuck around with Kena, but at the end of the day, she is my baby mom so I have to deal with her to a certain extent. Plus, it will work in my favor to be nice to her ass when I can so I can try to get some sort of joint custody when it comes to my Jr. I had been doing a damn good job by avoiding her ditzy ass but she was holding my son over my head and that shit was starting to eat at me. I missed damn near the entire first year of his life and now that I'm in his life, I didn't want to miss any more milestones because of Kena once again. This court shit doesn't work in a nigga's favor unless the mother is in agreeance with what the father is asking for, so having Kena on my side will work in my favor in the long run. I'm sure Erin wouldn't see it from my point of view so for the time being I'm going to keep this shit a secret from her. Knowing Erin's ass, she will automatically think I'm fucking around with Kena and be ready to cut a nigga off. I don't need Erin assuming anything and jumping on that bullshit right about now. Kena ain't going to give in when it comes to me that easily anyways. The more I avoid her and play her off, the harder the bitch goes. It's like she doesn't care about getting her ass beat or getting embarrassed in front of her girls.

Erin has been at the shop lately helping us get our paperwork and secretarial duties in order since we hadn't hired a permanent person for the position yet. I love the way my shorty steps in and helps out in any way possible. The only fucked up thing about having her at my place of business is when niggas come in, she be getting too much attention and that shit bothers me. I would hate to have to fuck a nigga up at my own business over his eyes wandering or words being too fresh when it comes to her. Come to think of it, Erin's little jealous ass been acting uptight on a nigga too. Whenever she sees a female come in the business for service she makes sure to be right in my face with the "babe this" or "bae that" like she's marking her territory. I find that shit to be cute for real because she has no problem letting a bitch know what's hers. Shit was going sweet though for everybody up until earlier today when Dupree's ex-bitch, Alisha, popped up at the job. She had been popping up around here a lot, but she just happens to be lucky enough to show her face whenever Erin isn't around. I guess today just wasn't one of Alisha's lucky days. As soon as Erin saw her she started giving not only me but Dupree the evil eye too. I'm sure she sent Renee a text informing her just because that's the type of relationship they share. My brother, on the other hand, looked like he was about to shit on himself when Alisha popped up and Erin was standing right there. Of course, Alisha caught the hint that she wasn't wanted around these parts today because she left shortly after she arrived, and I believe that was best. It's like as soon as she left, so did Erin, and she left with an attitude like I was the one who had an ex-bitch popping up at the shop. I texted her phone right after I realized she was gone, but she never responded. I called her when I felt like she was ignoring my texts just to see and of course, she sent my shit straight to the voicemail. Childish shit like this makes me rethink being in a fucking relationship to begin with.

"Yeah, bitch, suck that dick just like that," I grunted as Sariya sucked my dick as if she was sucking the soul out of me. Sariya was a little bitch I met up at the shop one day when she came in to get her car painted. She wasn't the baddest bitch but she would do for now. Plus, she was the head of her class when it came to topping a nigga off.

"Ummmm, daddy like this shit, umm," Sariya hummed while eyeing me as she did a trick with her mouth I had never felt before. Erin was cold when it came to pleasing a nigga with her mouth, but Sariya was one of a kind. I had never experienced head like hers in my life. No matter how hard I tried, I could never last longer than a few minutes when it came to Sariya's mouth lashings.

"Hell yeah, suck that shit. I'm 'bout to... Fuck, I'm 'bout to nut! Just like that. Fuck, grrrrrrr." Just like I expected, a nigga was a two-minute brotha once again. She slurped up all my nut and sucked until my shit got right back rock solid. As bad as I needed to get the fuck up outta her crib, there was no way I was leaving with my mans on rock hard. Sariya got off her knees and opened the condom she had placed on her coffee table. After placing the condom on my dick she gently slid down my pole like it was her personal toy for the moment. As soon as she felt that she had all of me inside of her, she took off, twerking her ass in circles and riding my dick like she was in a rodeo contest. The pussy was wet but the shit just wasn't tight like my girl's, but it would do. I was just trying to get a nut, nothing spectacular. If it wasn't for the tricks Sariya did, I think she would only be rated three stars out of five. Sariya threw her head back and leaned over so she was almost in a backbend on my lap, and continued to grind on my dick. I could tell by the way the pulsation in her pussy felt and the way her walls were contracting around my dick she was on the verge of cumming.

"Damn, daddy, this dick feels so good inside of me. Shit... ohhh, shit," she moaned and I laid back and rested my hands on her hips, while pumping upward, encouraging both of our orgasms to come sooner. Sariya's legs began to shake uncontrollably and I felt her cum seeping out onto my lap. Since baby girl got hers, it was time for me to hurry up and get my second round off so I could get my ass home. It was already after midnight and I'm sure Erin had been blowing my phone up, which was the reason I left it outside in my car. I stood up on my feet with my dick still inside of Sariya; she was basically upside down in a headstand. Gripping her hips tighter, I started fucking her wildly, just like I knew she wanted it. Before I knew it, I filled the condom with my seeds and let her down. Sariya's hair was all over the place and you could tell she had just got one of the best orgasms of her life from the way she was still shaking and panting. I made sure to wipe my dick off with a wash rag after I took a piss, before leaving her spot and heading home. Erin had yet to accuse me of some shit, but with the luck I have, tonight would be the night she would be on some Yvette from *Baby Boy* shit and want to smell my dick. I didn't use any soap when I wiped my dick off because that would be just as bad as the smell of another bitches' pussy.

As I expected, Erin had been blowing my phone up. Instead of calling her back, I powered my phone off and headed to her crib for the night. If my phone was powered off I could at least use the excuse that I didn't know she had been calling because I was out taking care of business and my phone died. I was thankful when I got to the house and Erin was in bed, fast asleep. I'm sure she would have some questions for me tomorrow, but I would deal with that headache then. Erin being asleep also gave me the opportunity to hop in the shower and go straight to sleep without needing to try to sneak to do anything without looking suspect. When I got out the shower, I placed my phone on the charger and powered it back on. Lying next to Erin and watching her sleep made a nigga feel bad for tipping out on her, but this relationship life is hard on a nigga. Any time Erin pisses me off, I feel the need to go get my whistle blown by the next bitch. I'm trying to steer clear of other bitches; I swear I really am. I just hope this shit doesn't catch up to me.

Shit, I can't lie, this road to recovery hasn't been easy but I can say I'm thankful to be almost back to my normal self. I won't be playing ball any longer but that's cool, I can accept that. I'm just thankful to still have my life after my accident. Since I won't be playing basketball this year, I got a job at a recreation center by the OSU campus, coaching teenagers. The location of my new job was perfect since I enrolled in fall courses at Ohio State University. Moving back home was in my future plans but I didn't think things would work out the way they have been. My support system being strong has made everything with my transition a lot easier. On top of having Rod still in my corner, there's Zion who is the coolest person ever. If I would have met him prior to the bullshit lie of a relationship I had with Coby, I would definitely be down with being with him. Considering all the shit I had just gone through mentally, I don't know if I can handle another relationship so soon. Granted, he is a good guy all around, now just isn't the time and I'm glad he respects that. Of course, Coby has reached out to me on numerous occasions. I just can't get with the fact that he was really undercover the entire time and the final ass whooping he put on me was just too much to bear. If I wouldn't have gotten beaten the way I did I wouldn't have stormed away from his house and gotten in the horrible car accident that I did so I partially blamed Coby for all I have been through recently. Coby had me fooled; he had the wool pulled over my eyes for sure. I would have never thought things would end the way they did between the two of us; Coby is like dating Mr. Hyde and Dr. Jekyll. He has two completely different personalities and there's no telling when either will resurface. The sad part is although I totally dislike him, I still love Coby. I don't know if it's because he is my first real boyfriend or the fact that he took my virginity. Whatever the reason may be that I still love him, I wish I could shake it already.

Tonight, Zion is coming into town to visit his grandma and we have plans for a date night. I enjoy spending time with him because everything we share is so different. Zion is so cool to be around and never once has he made me feel uncomfortable or like I was anything less than beautiful. I mean I really can clown with him and still not feel like either one of us is putting the other in the "friend zone". Dancing around my room, listening to Tamar Braxton's "Prettiest Girl" set the mood perfectly for how I felt about Zion. I had been searching for the perfect outfit to wear tonight for over an hour. Instead of dressing down like I normally do and rocking some flats or tennis shoes, I chose to rock a black maxi dress that I ordered offline with a pair of black and red strap up heels to show off my freshly manicured toes. I dressed up my outfit with gold accessories and a red clutch to bring out the red in my heels. The day had flown by because I really hadn't anticipated not being ready by the time Zion would be over to pick me up, yet I still had to put on my finishing touches. Zion had just sent me a text message letting me know he was downstairs talking with my parents. My hair was flawless as always and I had to be thankful for Erin suggesting that I get a few red highlights to complement my short cut. I'm definitely loving the look and I hope Zion will like it as well. I grabbed my Jimmy Choo perfume and sprayed all my hot spots, making sure to give just a hint of the fragrance, but not too much. I put a thin layer of my red MAC lipstick on and headed downstairs to meet Zion.

"Aww, shoot, watch out now!" my mother playfully announced my entrance into the room.

"Oh stop, Ma! I see yawl done got comfortable and didn't expect me to be coming down anytime soon," I said, eyeing Zion and my dad who were both having a shot of what I'm assuming was Cognac of some sort because of the color in their cups.

"Shit, knowing you, I wasn't expecting you to come down for another thirty to forty minutes. Don't worry, I ain't about to hold yawl up, we were only taking one quick drink. He's ready to go whenever you are, baby girl," my father stated.

"Well, hello Amoy, don't you look amazing!" I couldn't help but smile, showing all of my pearly whites at Zion's compliment. Eyeing him, I couldn't help but agree that he was looking damn good himself. If I hadn't thought about fucking this man's brains out by now, tonight would definitely be a different story.

"Thank you, Mr. Zion, you look amazing yourself. Are you ready to go?" I asked with the biggest smile plastered on my face.

"Yes, I sure am. Well, thanks for the drink Mr. Larry, and have a good night Mrs. Yolanda. I guess we will be getting out of here now." Zion said his goodbyes to my parents as he stood up and placed his shot glass in the kitchen sink.

"Ok, love yawl! Yawl may be sleep by the time I get back so don't try to wait up for me," I joked while looking at my parents. It seemed like no matter how old I was they still looked at me as their little girl.

"Oh, hush child. Yawl make sure you be careful and enjoy yourselves. Love you too," my mother said before waving me off.

"Love you too, Lee," my dad said before taking back his second shot.

Dinner was amazing. Zion made reservations for us at a restaurant called J. Alexanders and their food was on point. I ordered the Steak Maui with a Redlands Salad. When I tell you I smashed all of that food; there wasn't anything left on my plate to dispose of. Zion ordered the Redland Crab Cakes with Thai Kai salad. I was happy to see he wasn't a burger and fry type of guy and liked to try things outside of the box. We held a good conversation over dinner and to my surprise, without any interruptions of either of our phones. Zion's phone always goes off and I assume it is because of his line of work, but he always makes sure to inform whomever the callers are that he is with me and will contact them when he is finished. The only people who would be hitting my phone would normally be Rod or one of the girls, but they already knew I was on a date. Well, all except Rod. Although I still looked at Rod as my male best friend, he didn't hide the fact that he didn't care for the relationship I was establishing with Zion. I believe Rod may actually be jealous of the fact that I have someone who has my attention as more than a friend and it isn't him. During the course of dinner, Zion informed me that he wanted to go see a play that he had purchased tickets for. It seemed like as soon as I thought he couldn't be any more spontaneous he would come pulling tricks out of his hat. That was one of the reasons I enjoyed being with and around him any chance I could when he was in Columbus. This was the first play I had actually been to. Normally I just watched little plays and things on TV or on DVD, like Madea. The name of the play was "Married but Single", something I wouldn't expect a street nigga to be interested in. Even though Zion was very clean cut, well mannered, and polished, I know he's in the streets. Growing up with Kris, I can spot a hood nigga when I see him. Zion is just cut from a different cloth than normal street dudes from Columbus, being that he was born and raised down south.

The play was great and I wouldn't mind going to see more plays like it. Our night had been going so well and I wasn't ready for it to end, and neither was Zion. He told me he had booked a room at the Hilton downtown and would love for me to stay with him tonight. Since I wasn't trying to end our night so soon, I figured it wouldn't hurt to join him. I sent my mom a text message letting her know I wouldn't be home tonight so she wouldn't wake up worried when she realized I hadn't returned home. Since my car accident, I tried to let my parents know my whereabouts whenever I switched up my plans, just so they wouldn't be worrying about if I was ok or not. On the way to the room, Zion stopped by the liquor store and grabbed a bottle of Rosé. I had only tasted it once before so this was another new adventure to add to my list while being with Zion. The hotel was beautiful. Well, the hotel was nice and the view of downtown at night was beautiful. Zion came into the room and wasted no time breaking down a shell and rolling himself a blunt. I knew he smoked, but I adored the fact that he never smoked while out riding around or every ten minutes like some dudes do. There would be no way in hell I could tolerate being up under a weed head all day long, considering I had only smoked on occasions and never once picked it up as a habit. While Zion got his mind right, I decided to send a group text to the girls and let them know I would be staying with Zion.

Me: I'm with Zion for the night just so yawl know.

Erin: Ok boo. Enjoy the endcap of your date and hit me up with some good ass tea tomorrow, extra sugar, please.

Renee: Wrap it up, don't end up like me.

Netia: Better let that nigga knock the cobwebs off that shit.

Erin: Now you know that bitch shit way worse than some damn cobwebs. That nigga going to be fuckin' a born again virgin. Lee's scary ass going to fuck around and back out knowing her.

Me: Ctfu fuck all yawl hoes and goodnight.

One cup of Rosé turned into two and two turned into us finishing the bottle. I'm damn sure I caught a contact from the loud he was blowing in the air because I had the giggles and cottonmouth. We were so engaged in our conversation and laughs I hadn't even realized how much I had drank until I felt myself getting horny at all the little shit he would do that I never thought much of. Every time he coated his lips with his tongue, I found myself squeezing my legs close tighter.

"Man, you really are one of the coolest females I have ever come across. It's rare to find a female with her head on straight and not out here fucking her life up doing some weak shit. We really be having a good time together and I don't have to worry about you being up to nothing sneaky."

"I know. I love kicking it with you. I didn't expect you to be the way you are. I mean I'm not saying I expected you to be no lame or loser ass dude but from our conversation at the hospital when I first met you, I just thought you would be some nigga trying to get a quick nut and go. What has it been now like three or four months since we met and it's been nothing but coo' shit since day one."

"Hell yeah, I was just thinking that. Like damn, me and Amoy have never even had a simple disagreement in the time we been talking, which is rare. I was just waiting for some foul shit to pop out on me and turn me off but it hasn't. I'm really feeling you Lee and I can't even lie." Zion licked his lips once again while stroking his goatee, and I must say that shit turned me on. I couldn't help but lick my lips as well and smile. Zion stood about six feet tall, weighing about a hundred and eighty-five pounds, with nice, cut muscles. I'm sure he played some sort of sport during his younger days because of his masculine build. His brown skin looked amazing with his light brown eyes and shoulder length dreads with blonde tips. Zion has the cutest little lips, rocked golds on his bottom row of teeth that I couldn't wait to shine and he has a scar on the left side of his face; I'm sure that has some crazy story behind it. Zion reached over and started massaging my knee. As bad as I wanted him to back away, I was enjoying the feeling. I didn't want to cross the line with him and everything went south, but the feeling and mood were just right. It had been so long since I felt a man's touch and it actually felt damn good. When he felt me begin to relax, he took that as the green light and continued, while inching his hand a little higher with each motion. I accidently let out a soft moan and it was over with from there. Zion leaned forward and started rubbing his soft lips against the side of my face. I leaned my head to the side, allowing him to nibble on my neck a little. I felt my panties getting wetter by the second as he placed several kisses from my lips to my neck repeatedly. While kissing on me, he moved his hand toward my center and I slowly opened my legs wider, allowing him access to my love nest. When Zion's hands reached my panties, he ripped my thong in one swift motion without me having to lift my ass, and surprisingly it didn't hurt. The feeling of his fingers toying around with my clit made me sit up straight and arch my back, while throwing my head back and enjoying the feeling. He was so gentle, but it was perfect. I liked that he was taking his time getting to know my body, along with how each touch caused my body to react to him. When he inserted his two fingers into me I could have sworn I began to cum, but it may have just been from the anticipation of feeling something inside of me after so long. The way Zion moved his fingers in and out of me while rubbing his thumb over my clit caused my body to twitch. I felt him lifting my dress and I couldn't even assist him. It seemed as if my body was just floating on air and he was taking care of it on his own. I won't complain because he took his time and I'm a grown woman. If I didn't want him to do any of the things he was doing I should have never got to this level with him. Zion pushed me back onto the couch and pulled me closer to him. Before I knew it he was pushing his dreads to the back and was going head first between my legs. The feeling of his moist tongue twirling around my clit was enough to make a bitch fall in love. I mean Coby ate the box plenty of times but it never felt this good. The moans that were escaping my lips I couldn't hold in and at any point I was scared that me calling out his name or daddy would come out my mouth. His tongue was doing tornadoes in my love nest and I now knew what Lil Kim meant when she said that a nigga had a hurricane tongue in the lyrics of one of her old songs. If his dick brings any pleasure like his tongue, there is no way I would only let this be a one-night stand. "Oh, ohhhhhh, ohhhh my God, Z. This feels so goo... good," I moaned aloud. He gripped my ass cheeks and pulled me into his face, causing him to feast even deeper. Zion started moving his head up and down, practically fucking me with his tongue. I reached forward to grab his head and pull his dreads for leverage because I needed something to hold with the way my body was squirming. "I'mm cummm... cummin', I'm cummin'! It feels... yess it feels, ahhhhhhh," I said as I spilled all of my juices onto his face. As soon as I let my orgasm out, Zion sat up and looked into my eyes with a stare I had never witnessed before.

"Are you ok, can I go ahead?" Zion softly asked while nodding his head down and looking at his rock hard dick sticking through his pants.

"Umm hum," was all I could say because I honestly couldn't wait to feel what he had to offer. Zion removed his pants and slowly rubbed the tip of his dick up and down my creases. I didn't see the actual size of his dick outside of his pants print because my head was back and my eyes were closed, but from what I could feel, he was working with a monster. I just hope I could take it like I needed to. I tensed up when I felt him at the entrance of my hole. When he got the tip inside, I felt like I was losing my virginity all over again. The pain was worse than I remember from the first time with Coby. As Zion slowly stroked in and out of me, the feeling eased up and became more pleasurable than painful. Once I noticed he had all of it inside of me I began to pump upward and fuck him back, matching every thrust. Zion licked his lips before biting down on his bottom one, looking sexy as hell.

"Cum for me, Amoy. Let me feel you cum all on this dick." Biting down on the side of my bottom lip, I had every intention of cumming for him like he requested.

"Z, don't stop, I'm 'bout to cum, baby. Shit baby, I'm about to cum. Keep on, right there." I didn't need to instruct him on what or how to keep hitting because once he found my G-spot, he hadn't let up since, but I still felt like telling him how I felt.

"Grrrr, shit Amoy. Fuck, grrrrr." Zion let out a loud grunt and we were cumming together. Zion leaned down and kissed me on the lips passionately. We allowed our tongues to play for a second before he lifted up off of me and grabbed my hand, leading me to the shower. Zion and I showered together and went at it for a few more rounds before returning back to the sleeping area of the room and cuddling up. Laying in Zion's arms completely naked, I didn't have an insecurity in this world. Even with all the scars from my accident I still felt flawless laying in his arms. "Amoy, I enjoyed every minute of tonight with you and I know neither of us is ready to take it to the next level but I will say this; I don't think I can allow you to share that pussy with the next nigga."

"You're right, Z. We aren't ready to go there just yet, but I can promise you I won't be fucking around with no other niggas, just promise me you won't be sharing that dick like it belongs to the community." Zion laughed at my comment before kissing the nape of my neck.

"Now one thing I can assure you of is this dick ain't for everybody," Zion said and shortly after I could hear soft snores escaping his lips. With Zion fast asleep, holding my waist tight, I drifted off to sleep comfortably in his arms shortly after.

Since that night I shared with Zion, I can't lie and say he hasn't been on my mind every day. I hate that he lives so far away but I guess that's a good thing because after the night we shared it would be all bad if we were able to spend every day with each other. As bad as I would try to avoid catching feelings for him, it would be damn near impossible if he lived any closer. Not only did I need to mentally prepare myself for the fall semester that was approaching at a fast pace, I needed to focus on Lee and not a relationship. Rod and I have been having little lunch dates as he calls them, but to me, it's more so just eating lunch with my best friend. Instead of Rod moving here to Columbus like he was initially planning when I first got into my car accident, he just comes up here for weeks at a time and travels back and forth between West Virginia and Ohio like it's down the street or around the corner. Tomorrow is the day of Rod's sister's baby shower and he has not only invited me but Renee, Erin and Netia as well. This will be the first time I actually get to meet his family in person. He passes messages between us whenever we are on the phone like saying hello or asking how the other is doing, but nothing more nothing less. Since I didn't personally know Rod's sister, I decided to purchase a hundred-dollar gift card from me and whoever decided to tag along with me. Erin would probably be the lucky candidate that has to sit in complete strangers' faces and pretend to have a good time since Renee wasn't feeling too well and Netia was going out of town to meet up with some new boo she had just met. Renee had been sick a lot lately. It seems like since she came out and told everyone she was pregnant she's been sick. This baby is really kicking her ass worse than what Sanai did when she was pregnant with her. I hope it's over with after her first trimester because I don't know how much more throwing up that girl will be able to take. Monday is the first day of the fall semester so I might as well do all I can before classes start because after Monday, I'll be back with my head in the books and limited time for anything else on the side.

"Girl, this baby shower is the bomb! They had to spend a fortune on all this nice shit. You better believe I'm going to be snapping pictures and taking note of ideas to steal for Renee's baby shower," Erin whispered in my ear as we walked towards an empty table in the corner. She was right; the decorations were beautiful and the "Royal prince" theme was so cute. The colors royal blue and gold looked nice together. There was everything from balloon arches to little gold crowns everywhere. Whoever paid for this baby shower didn't spare their pockets any. There were little personalized napkins with the name Roi'al on them; I'm guessing that's what they were naming the baby.

"Bitch, you're crazy, but you're right, this shit is laid the fuck out. I knew Rod wasn't broke, so I assumed his family had a little bit of paper, but damn. You would think this is really for a royal family or some shit," I replied back to Erin.

"Shit, bitch you fuckin' with the wrong nigga. You need to be fuckin' with Rod if his money long like that. Or shit, if his inheritance is long like that. I mean it ain't like you trying to really be with Zion no how; you just stringing that nigga along and you know it. Where the fuck is Rod at anyways, and where is his sister? How the fuck we sitting in a baby shower full of strangers and the one person we do know isn't even here." Erin's fucking mouth was going a mile a minute and I couldn't help but laugh at her.

"Shut up, hoe. I just texted him and he said he is on his way in now. I guess he and his sister must have rode together or something." Just as I said that we heard the music start playing and in came Rod, followed by a pregnant Nyla, holding hands with Mark.

"Bitch, what the fuck? What type of shit is this? Did you know that Nyla was Rod's sister? Oh hell no, I can't believe I let you talk me into coming to this shit. Nice or not, ain't no way in hell we should be sitting in this bitch. And to think, this nigga had the nerve to invite Renee. What if Nae would have come, it would have been a bunch of shit popping off in this hoe's baby shower." Erin was going off and I'm sure somebody heard her because she was no longer whispering.

"Hell no I ain't know Nyla was his fucking sister! Bitch, do you really think I would have invited my sister after all the shit Mark put her through? Shit, do you really think I would have come to this shit my damn self. Whoever yawl got beef with or problems with, so the fuck do I. It ain't never been no funny shit when it comes to outsiders and that shit ain't about to start now. I'm 'bout to give Rod this gift card and we getting the fuck out of here because I don't know if I'm going to be able to fake the funk and smile in that nigga Mark's face. You know I don't do too well with pretending."

"Coo', cause if not, we going to need back up in this bitch for sure cause we are definitely outnumbered. We surrounded by their fucking family and friends, not ours. I mean like Bone Crusher, bitch, I ain't never scared, but if I ain't gotta get my ass unnecessarily jumped I'm not about to," Erin said popping her neck from side to side with a smile on her face. I swear this hoe has some missing screws.

"You know what, better yet, I'm not giving them motherfuckers shit. I can give this gift card to my sister. Let me text Rod and tell him that we have to go and to meet me outside." Right as I said that, I looked up and Rod was walking in my direction with his sister in tow. I let out a sigh and shook my head. *I be damn,* I thought to myself.

"Hey, Lee, this is my sister, Nyla. Nyla, this is the infamous Lee I have told you so much about." The smile on Nyla's face disappeared right along with the one I was giving Rod. Now that I look at the two of them beside each other, they looked exactly alike. How could I not put two and two together? I mean Nyla isn't the most common name but damn. We say Columbus is small, but now I'm seeing it's not just Columbus.

"Well hello, Lee, how are you doing?" Nyla said in a slick tone. *I know this bitch ain't trying to be funny cause she's pregnant, cause she can still get these hands with no problem*, I thought to myself.

"I'm good! What's up, Nyla, how are you?" I said, matching the same smart ass tone she gave me.

"Am I missing something here? Do yawl know each other already or something?" Rod asked.

"Actually, we do. Nyla is my sister's ex-nigga's new thing for the time being. But I called you over here to tell you we are about to leave and I'll get up with you later. This whole thing ain't sitting right with me and you know I'm not down with no funny bullshit," I told Rod while grabbing my clutch and standing to my feet, preparing to leave.

"Damn, I don't even know what to say. Had I known that I would have never put either of you in this type of predicament. My fault y'all," Rod explained himself before I walked away. When Erin and I reached the door, we ran dead into Mark's lame ass. When he saw us it was almost like he had witnessed two ghosts standing before him. As bad as I wanted to reach up and punch that weak ass nigga dead in his mouth, I chose to walk right past him and let him get his when the time came. Now wasn't the time and this baby shower sure wasn't the fucking place.

"Bitch, can you believe this shit? I'm glad Renee didn't come with us. This entire situation could have turned out completely different."

"Man, bitch I'm so fucking pissed! I don't even know what to say. I could just fuck up every one of them right about now." I was so mad my hand was shaking. That's something that happened when I got upset or wanted to fight or do something and I couldn't. If it wasn't for Nyla being pregnant, I would've punched that bitch right in her shit in front of everybody there, just on the strength that I know she said some slick shit to Renee concerning Mark and my niece that day at the grocery store, which wasn't her fucking place. Yeah, Renee is a grown woman but since I know Renee isn't going to put the bitch in her place like she needs to be, I feel like I should be the one to do it.

"I know you are pissed, but just calm down because as of right now that hoe is untouchable and she knows it because she's pregnant. Don't worry, every dog has their day and she won't be pregnant forever. Trust and believe when she does drop her load, it's over for that hoe," Erin replied.

After seeing Lee leaving my son's baby shower, I expected to see her brother and his sidekicks show up and try to prove a point, but I was wrong. I'm actually thankful they didn't come because I didn't want anything to ruin that day for Nyla. On top of it being her first child, her entire family was there and it has been hard enough to get them to accept me, considering she conceived my son out of wedlock. I didn't need them looking at me like some hoodlum too. Our baby shower turned out real nice and Nyla's parents paid a pretty penny to make sure their first grandchild would be coming into this world with a bang. We received so many gifts and gift cards we won't be needing to buy anything out of pocket for at least the first year or so. I'm thankful that we did get so much because we hadn't purchased anything prior and we don't have much longer before Roi'al will be here. I wanted my first son to carry my name and be a junior, but Nyla stressed how her family didn't agree with him being a junior if she didn't have my last name. So needless to say, we agreed on Roi'al and I chose the spelling, wanting him to be different. Our son's name definitely fit him because that's exactly how he was being treated already and he hadn't even blessed this earth with his presence yet. I can see now he's going to be spoiled beyond a doubt. Nyla's parents are taking things overboard with the shit they are buying if you ask me. Nyla says that the only reason I feel this way is because I've been through the beginner parent phase with Sanai, but even with Sanai we didn't buy some of the unnecessary shit I see them bringing over. But shit it's their money, not mine, so fuck it.

"Mark, do you hear me talking to you, boy?" my mother yelled while throwing an oven mitts at my head, snapping me out of my daydream.

"Nah, mom, what did you say?"

"I asked your simple ass when you're going to work this shit out with Renee? I miss my grandbaby. There's no way she should've been put in the middle of y'alls stupid bullshit to begin with. I thought Renee was better than this. I can't believe she's kept her from us this long." My mom was pissed and I could tell by her tone. She had been asking me a lot more lately about getting Sanai and if Renee had changed her mind about letting her come with me, but I just brushed her off. The truth was I hadn't told my mom Renee and I was going back and forth about Sanai being mine or not and that was the real reason why Renee took Sanai away from us. The only reason I hadn't told my mom is because I still feel like Sanai is mine and until I have the proof myself, I'm not going off of what they tell me. Shit, anybody can lie, including Renee and her bitch ass nigga.

"I called her but she must have changed her number or some shit. I'm just going to stop by there on my way home tonight." Thinking about it now was starting to piss me off all over again because this petty bullshit is childish. I've been in Sanai's life since the day Renee found out she was pregnant and if she was out thoting then she should've never allowed it to be a secret this long. I don't give a fuck about what she or her nigga says, I'm going to see my daughter. My mind is made up; I'm going over there tonight, welcomed or not.

"Good, because this shit is draggin' out for too long and I'm muthafuckin' tired of it," my mom said before picking her can of Budweiser back up and taking a swig. I couldn't help but laugh. Even though the situation wasn't funny, my mother's ratchet ass ways were a trip.

"Alright, mom, I'm about to get out of here. I gotta stop and grab

Nyla's prescription before the CVS pharmacy closes. I'll be by here tomorrow." I kissed my mom on her forehead before leaving her house.

Grabbing Nyla's prenatal prescription prior to heading to Renee's apartment, I felt my anger building thinking about how difficult she was making this shit for me. So what I kicked her ass a few times; she deserved that shit each and every time in my opinion. The way Renee feels about me personally ain't got shit to do with me being a father to my daughter. Pulling into the complex, I didn't see Renee's car but I did see that nigga Dupree's Dodge Charger, so I debated on whether I should wait until tomorrow to come back. When I thought about how long it's been since I've seen Sanai, I decided to go ahead and shoot my shot by heading up to knock on her door. Before I exited my car I made sure I grabbed my piece, just in case that nigga Dupree was here instead of Renee, considering his car was parked here. Walking up, I could hear laughter coming from Renee's apartment. I'm glad I didn't turn around and leave because she was inside, laughing and enjoying her night like she wasn't affecting my life by keeping my child away from me.

Boom! Boom! Boom! Hearing whoever was inside with Renee and her having a good ol' time pissed me off to the max! I couldn't even be considerate and knock like the average person would when coming by to visit. There's no point in me being nice if she wanted to play these stupid ass games.

"WHO IS IT?" Renee yelled from the other side of the door.

"MARK. OPEN THIS FUCKING DOOR, RENEE!" I yelled back, not giving a fuck which neighbor heard me or looked out.

"Mark, what do you want? There's no reason for you to be here," Renee questioned me instead of opening the door.

BOOM, BOOM, BOOM! I banged even harder than I did the first time since she wasn't getting the point. I didn't come over here to play with her about my fucking daughter. "OPEN THIS GOTDAMN DOOR! NOW!" I yelled once again.

"Open the door, Renee!" I heard a male voice instruct her from the opposite side. I removed my piece from my hip and took it off safety. Renee opened the door slowly, with fear written all over her face.

"Mark, what do you need? I've told you there is no reason for you to be around us and you have gone too far coming over here banging on the door like this." Renee's voice was no longer in a yelling tone. She hadn't opened the door completely so I was unable to see who the male voice belonged to. I pushed the door open wider and saw Dupree sitting on the couch comfortably with his shirt off and some basketball shorts like this was his home. The sight of him caused my blood to boil. Forcing my way into the apartment, I caught both of them off guard.

"Nigga! What's up?" Dupree asked in a stern tone while standing to his feet like he was ready for whatever.

"That's what I'm trying to find out. What's up?" I asked, stepping all the way inside and pushing the door closed. "You standing up like you 'bout to do some shit or something. Where the fuck is my daughter?"

"Bitch nigga, that's my fucking daughter and what I'm about to do is let your ass right the fuck back out. Nae didn't invite you in so the shit you just pulled was real disrespectful." This nigga was talking to me like he was my muthafucking dad or some shit and it caused me to feel some type of way on the inside. I raised my gun and pointed it at him before speaking. Renee started yelling and jumped in front of me, trying to de-escalate the situation, but it was too late.

"Oh my GOD, Mark, no! Please, just leave! Sanai is here and this has gone too far! Just please leave or I'm calling the police," Renee screamed with tears pouring from her eyes.

"Bitch, move! What you about to do, protect this fuck ass nigga? Yawl both got life fucked up if yawl think yawl 'bout to live life happily ever after like some big happy family with my fucking daughter! I let this nigga get away with the shit yawl pulled at your parents, so this shit is way overdue." I was so focused on Renee I didn't see Dupree lunging towards me until his fist connected with my jaw. He started raining blows on me. Before I could retaliate, I had fallen backward onto the floor. I managed to not drop my gun in the process of falling and I didn't even see where I was aiming, I just pulled the trigger, firing shots, not giving a fuck where the bullets landed. As far as I was concerned, he and Renee both deserved a few of the shots. There was no particular target at this time in my defense. I heard Renee scream and I saw the nigga Dupree fall to the floor. Renee kept screaming and crying but I was unable to make out what she was saying because all I saw was red at the moment. When I was able to look around the living room, there was blood everywhere. Instead of continuing to look around to see the damage I caused, I turned and ran out the front door toward the direction of my car. I'm not sure exactly where I hit the nigga but I know I needed to get the fuck out of there. I wasn't expecting the situation to get that bad that fast, but it was too late now. I hope the nigga dies! Renee and Sanai are my family and he was the only thing in the way of me having them to myself. I hopped in my car and sped away from Renee's place. I did no less than eighty-five miles per hour toward Nyla's.

Walking in the front door, Nyla was sitting on the couch, Indian style, eating out the carton of vanilla ice cream. She damn near tripped over her own feet, jumping up and heading in my direction when she looked over at me.

"Baby, what happened to you? Oh my God, please tell me what happened. I'm calling the police right now! Who did this to you?" Nyla asked with tears beginning to spill from her eyes.

"NO, NO, don't call the police!" was all I could say. If she called the police, there was no question about it; I was going to be going straight to jail. Ain't no passing go or collecting two hundred dollars, this is real life. I had just forced entry into Renee's apartment, shot her nigga, and possibly her too. I'm not even sure where I shot him. For all I know, he could be dead. No matter how you looked at it, I was guilty of committing more than one crime. Fucked up thing is I feel no remorse for what I just did.

"Mark, what do you mean don't call the police? You have blood all over you and your face still has blood coming from somewhere. I can't even tell where you're hurt or where the blood is coming from. Oh my God, Mark! What the fuck happened? Please tell me something," Nyla cried.

"I went to see about my daughter, since Renee changed her number and refused to allow me in my daughter's life. I'm tired of this shit so I went over to her place and got into it with her bitch ass boyfriend. We ended up fighting and I shot him. The nigga thought I was going to allow him to talk to me crazy so I started whooping his ass right there in her front room and before you know it, my anger took over and I shot the nigga before I left. I don't know if it's all my blood you see or both of ours." I lied a little but shit, Nyla didn't need to know I shot the nigga because he was really whooping my ass for coming at him and Renee the way I did.

"No, Mark, tell me you didn't just do that! Mark, you didn't! Why would you shoot him? The police are going to come, Mark, I know they are! You're going to be in trouble, Mark. Why? Why, Mark? Why would you do something so stupid? You're going to go to jail! I can't believe this!" Nyla was pacing the floor, crying and holding her head like she was losing her mind. Shit, I should've been the one pacing the floor and holding my head. As far as I was concerned, I could be looking at facing some serious prison time, depending on if the nigga was killed by the shots fired or not.

"Nyla, calm the fuck down and shut up! I need to figure this shit out right now and you're not helping any by screaming and crying," I shouted at her, causing her to cry even harder.

"Mark, I can't calm down, I'm scared! What if the police come and take you to jail? What if his friends and family come for you to retaliate or something? Mark, I'm due here soon. We have a son to worry about and all of this is not the type of situation I want to bring him into the world around. I'm scared. We got to get out of here, Mark. I know somebody is going to come looking for you, I just know they are. Whether it's the police or his peoples. We got to go, Mark. We got to go!" Nyla said before turning to head upstairs. Nyla was right, we did have to get out of here, but where the fuck are we going to go? I can't go to my mom's house because that's the first place anyone would go looking for me. We couldn't go to her parents' house and include them in what's going on. The only options we had was the place her brother had for when he was in Columbus or a hotel. Nyla is going to have to figure out a lie to tell her brother so he doesn't become suspicious if we go there so, for now, a hotel is the safest place we can go until my money gets low.

RENEE

Mark's ass has officially gone crazy. When he popped up at my house I never thought things would get out of hand the way they did, especially with my daughter sleeping upstairs. Had I known things were going to take a turn for the worse in the way they did, I would have called the cops as soon as I knew it was him at the door. I didn't even plan on actually opening the door, but Dupree advised me to. Mark just wasn't getting the point that Sanai is really not his daughter. I can't help but blame myself for all of this shit happening at the hands of Mark. I should've never let him believe that Sanai was his daughter for so long, but I honestly didn't know from day one who she was, so I just went along with Mark since that's who I was with. Mark caused me to lose my job, fucked up my car, fucked up my apartment with the blood from him and Dupree and he had shot Dupree in three different places. Two shots were only bullet grazes and one bullet went through his shoulder completely, without hitting anything inside. I'm so thankful that Dupree wasn't harmed seriously and that Sanai remained asleep while all of the commotion was going on. I would hate for her to have had to witness such a scene at such a young age. I don't even argue in front of her, let alone fight and see bloodshed. Since none of Dupree's bullet wounds were life-threatening or critical, they patched him up the same night and sent him home. Instead of us returning to my apartment, we went to Dupree's place and have been staying here ever since. Ever since Dupree and I have been together, he had been staying at my place, so his place was basically empty and reminded you of a bachelor pad for sure. It was only temporary so I didn't complain. Plus, there was no way I was taking my daughter back over to a place that was a crime scene.

Of course, the police were involved when I had to call 911 for help. As bad as Dupree didn't want me to get the police involved, I went against his orders to make sure we would be doing things the right way. The police said that they would take care of Mark, but I knew Dupree, Dame and Kris would get him before the police would have a chance to. Dame was beyond worth when I called to inform him of the situation and Kris about lost it before he knew the details of what happened. It's safe to say that everyone is beyond tired of Mark and his antics. Either way, Mark is fucked for that stunt he pulled. I also filed a protection order against Mark so that way if he did come back around we would be covered on our end legally. He had no reason to come around; Sanai isn't his and I'm not going back to him. If I was ever considering it before, my mind is for sure made up now. Mark has become too demented for me and those shots he fired could have hit Dupree or me. If one would've gone through the floors or walls my baby could've been hit as well. There's no excuse for his behavior, especially after I warned him that my daughter was home. Bullets don't have names and Mark had no aim; shots were just being fired in all directions carelessly.

Dupree had been off of work recovering for a few weeks and soon he would be back to the old Dupree. I could tell him being unable to do some of the things he was used to caused frustration, but he was doing a good job masking it whenever I was around. Since he couldn't work as hard, I had been going into his office, helping out as much as possible to lighten the level of stress and workload for when he returned. My pregnancy is still going smooth as far as the baby is concerned, besides the constant morning sickness, but with Dupree being down I had to put my big girl panties on and push my sickness to the back burner. I will be beyond happy when this pregnancy is over. I didn't have half this much vomiting when I was pregnant with Sanai.

"Baby, your phone hasn't stopped going off since I walked in, do you want me to answer it?" I yelled upstairs to Dupree. I had only been home for about thirty minutes and his phone has been going off nonstop. If it was a close friend or relative and it was an emergency they knew to call my phone, so whoever it was wasn't close, but it had to be important to continue to call after he hadn't answered the first few times.

"Yeah, go ahead," Dupree responded. He had just gotten out of the shower and was getting dressed. Although we were together, we still didn't answer each other's phones without permission. There was never a reason for us to need the other's phone because we had our own phone, on top of having just that much trust between us. When I grabbed Dupree's phone to answer it, the number wasn't saved so I assumed it was a customer or someone trying to reach him in regards to his business.

"Hello?" I answered in the politest tone possible, although I was agitated by their continuous calls.

"Umm, hey! Hello, is Dupree available?" a female hesitated to respond, but asked for him by his first name, which is something many customers didn't do.

"I'm sorry, Dupree isn't available to come to the phone at the moment. May I ask who's calling?"

"Yeah, this is Alisha. Can you let him know to call me back as soon as possible, please? It's very important! Is this Renee?" This bitch knew exactly who it was. Now I know why the caller continued to call back to back; it was his ex trying to get in contact with him.

"Yeah, this is Renee and I'll let him know you called."

"Thanks, hun!" Alisha said and laughed before hanging up. If I ain't know any better I would think she was trying to be funny by asking who I was, then laughing when I confirmed it was me. As bad as I wanted to ask her why the fuck she was blowing up my man's phone, I left it alone and waited to let Dupree know she was the person who kept calling and see his response.

"Who was it, babe?" Dupree asked as he came down the stairs, joining me in the kitchen.

"Alisha, all one hundred times!" I responded sarcastically. Dupree smirked before responding.

"What you mean all one hundred times? Did she really call that many times or you just talking shit?" he asked.

"No, she really did just call for thirty minutes straight, back to back. I'm not sure of the exact number of times, but it was far too many if you ask me. She told me to tell you to call her as soon as possible because it's important."

"Aww, ok. I don't know why she felt the need to call that many times. I haven't talked to that girl in God knows how long. I wonder if it has something to do with her baby," Dupree said while rubbing his hand over his waves as if he was a little nervous.

"I don't know what it was, but I hope it really is important by the way she just blew your shit down."

"Where's my phone, babe? I'll find out what it is she wants and if it's really important or not." I handed Dupree his phone and turned my attention towards him so I could see why the hell she was calling so much. Dupree called her and although I couldn't hear her, I still listened to him question her about the reason she called and if there was something wrong. Whatever she was saying couldn't have been that important because he ended the call rather quickly. As soon as Dupree ended the call and placed his phone in his short's pocket, I wasted no time.

"Did she say what was so urgent?" I asked.

"Yeah, but nothing for real. She said she is supposed to be getting induced Friday and would like for me to be there." Dupree was now rubbing his hands over his waves once again and looking as if his entire mood had changed. I was unable to read him fully, but I know he wasn't the most excited by their conversation.

"Why would she want you there? I thought you said she told you it wasn't your baby?" My heart would be broken in pieces if the baby was his. I know what they had was before we worked things out and made "us" official, but I don't know how I could handle Dupree having another female as his baby mom. I was supposed to be the only woman who birthed his children and I didn't want to share any title I had with Dupree with another.

"Originally she did say that, but now she claims she only said it out of anger, but I don't know honestly. I mean if it is my baby I'm going to be there for it. I'm not going to leave my child high and dry, but I don't want to deal with no foolish shit with her if that's what's going to come along with it."

"So what is that supposed to mean for us?" I asked, feeling my eyes begin to water. I don't know if it was the pregnancy to blame for me becoming emotional so quickly or the fact that if the baby did belong to Dupree, I would now have to share him with another female.

"What you mean? What does that mean for us? Renee, I'm not about to leave you if I father her child. That has nothing to do with our relationship. Now if the baby is mine it will mean you will have to accept my other child and it will be around, but as far as we are concerned, we aren't about to end just because Alisha's baby may be mine. Shit, we don't even know as of right now. She's been missing in action for months now so until the baby gets here and a DNA test proves it's mine, don't worry about it. Ok?"

"Ok. You say that now Dupree but when the baby gets here, she's really going to blow your phone up and want you around all the time. She just called for a half an hour straight just to tell you that little bit of information, so imagine how much she will call if the baby is yours. I would never not accept your child, but I just don't want our relationship to be affected because of your baby mom. You see how Dame and his baby mom go through shit and it causes drama between him and Erin. I just don't want that type of stress or drama to come into our relationship." Dupree let out a loud sigh and I could tell he was beginning to get frustrated by this conversation, but I needed him to see where I was coming from. I mean here I am standing in front of him almost four months pregnant and crying over the fact that his ex could possibly be delivering a baby that may be his in less than a week. Our entire relationship we worked so hard for could just crumble at any moment if that DNA test reads the baby is his. Dupree is not looking at it from my point of view simply because it's a possibility of it being his own flesh and blood, but I know females and I know

Alisha was just being funny when she called, so it would only get worse.

"Damn, Renee, why do you have to make this situation sound so fucking bad when we don't even know anything for sure as of right now. Another thing, don't ever compare our relationship or me to my brother and his shit. We are two different people and what we have is one of a kind. It's not like any relationship he has. Like I said, stop stressing and let this shit go for now." I simply shook my head, wiped my tears from my face and turned around to finish where I left off with preparing our food.

I mean am I being selfish for feeling the way that I do? I know Mark has caused nothing but drama and problems for Dupree and me, but this situation is different in my eyes. Or is it? Maybe I'm just seeing it this way because I know for a fact Dupree is a good man and I've fucked up with him in the past, so I don't want another woman to luck up on what's mine. I can't catch a fucking break, I swear! Dupree and I are happy with what we have and don't have any problems, but when you include our ex's into the equation our relationship is just a big ball of drama and problems.

The last week or so I've been walking around in my own funk. Since the day Alisha called and announced her induction, shit has been different in our house. I could sense Dupree's on edge attitude and I was honestly more depressed than I had been in a long while. We were allowing this situation to tear at our relationship without even having the results of the DNA test yet. I couldn't help but think that my little family was about to be torn apart just as fast as we got on track. Whenever Dupree wasn't home, I would find myself crying to myself just thinking about it. That Friday Alisha was induced, Dupree went to the hospital and stayed there with her the entire day. Although he sent me text messages and called, I still felt hurt by him being there for her. Maybe it was because he wasn't able to be home comforting me, or because he wasn't there when our daughter was born because of my own selfishness and stupidity. Alisha ended up having a little boy and that shit hurt. If it was his, she would have his first son. We still hadn't found out what I'm having yet, but I'm no longer excited to find out now. They swabbed for DNA the day the baby was born, but the results of the testing weren't back yet, so we are still unsure. The baby is still nameless because he for one is still in the hospital being treated for infant jaundice. The second reason is because of course Alisha wants him to be a junior and Dupree refused to give him his name until it is proven that he is in fact 99.9% his son. As bad as I wanted Dupree to just cut all ties with Alisha and for her baby not to be his, I knew he wouldn't. Dupree is not the type of guy to walk away from his child. It sounds selfish, but I can only think about my little family right now. Their situation really isn't any better than my situation with Dupree and Mark in the beginning, only this time, I'm on the outside looking in. Just like I didn't know exactly who Sanai's dad was at first, neither does she, so I really can't judge Alisha, as bad as I want to.

"Dame, I swear if I read one more fucking subliminal message from this hoe about you and this weak ass girl I'm going to her house personally and fucking her up. You keep defending this bitch whether you see it that way or not. There is no excuse for her to be posting you as her MCM or bragging about what you do for her. It's no problem what you do for your son with her, but taking care of that bitch is another story."

"Erin, go on with that bullshit, it's too late to be arguing over this dumb shit right now. I'm tired and I got to be up early. I'm really not trying to hear this shit at all tonight!" Dame said as he threw his dirty clothes in the hamper. He had just come in the house and he was right, it was late, but that was his fault. If he would have come home sooner, then we wouldn't be having this conversation so late.

"So the fuck what it's late! I'm sick of biting my tongue and not addressing the shit I see or hear because you claim it's nothing between you two. And then you complaining about being tired. Nigga, you ain't the only one who is tired and has to be up early in the morning. You're tired because you choose to continue to come home late as fuck every other night like you don't have to be up and at work in the morning. Why is it that she feels the need to make you her Man Crush

Monday and brag about what you did for her if you ain't fucking with the nasty bitch? Huh? Just answer that question. Hello! Cat got your tongue now?"

"No, but it would be nice if some cat did have my tongue instead of having to argue with you about some shit that's not even relevant. No, I'm not fucking with her like that and I have no control over that bitch making me her Man Crush nothing. Shit, I don't even have anything on social media. Maybe she's doing that shit cause she knows it's going to piss you off like it is."

"Whatever, Dame. You think I'm so naive that I don't know when there is some truth behind the shit she says. Then you keep on going around the fact that she says you taking care of her and doing shit for her. So is it fucking true or not? Are you tricking on this bitch? Huh, Dame, are you? You know what, don't even answer that fucking question; I already know the answer. It's coo'. Keep playing with me and these other bitches if you want to. I know one damn thing, you better not bring me nothing back while you fucking with that herpes and everything else having ass bitch." I was no longer lying in bed watching TV like I was when he first walked in. I was now standing to my feet, yelling, pointing in his direction and punching my fist out of frustration. Something told me in my gut that Dame was cheating, I just had no solid proof. A woman's intuitions are always right and there was no reason for him to be out all times of night like some nickel and dime hustler when he had two legit jobs besides the hustling shit.

"Erin, I'm not going to tell your simple ass again. I don't feel like going through this tonight. Shut the fuck up. I don't want to argue, I just want to lay in bed next to my woman and go to fucking sleep without all this extra shit. You ask shit then turn around and give yourself an answer like some damn psychic. You want answers, I give them to you, then when they aren't what you want to hear you assume whatever it is you want to. Yes, I gave the bitch some money; you act like it took away from you. I only gave her some fucking money to keep her off my damn back and be coo' when we go to court, but I guess I'm in the wrong for doing it. Or, are you mad I didn't tell you about it? Either way, you wouldn't have agreed with me doing it. So what now, are you done?" Dame asked while lying down on the bed and turning his back toward me.

"No, I'm not done. I'll be done when I'm good and fucking ready. You right, I don't agree with it. You're not her fucking man so whoever she fucking should be the one cashing her out. Let me walk in this bitch with some money from another nigga, you would blow my fucking cap back and never let me hear the end of it, but it's ok for you to do for the next bitch. When is the last time you fucked her, Dame? Just be honest, nigga. Why lie? I know you're doing something, just keep it one hundred. You such a real nigga, keep it real with me then." Dame just ignored me like I wasn't still standing here asking him a question and waiting for his lying ass to answer them.

"Hello? So now I'm talking to myself, huh? You know what, fuck you, Dame. You and that nasty bitch can have each other. Yawl can keep that herpes between yawl; I'm coo' on that shit. You do you and I'll do me, it's coo'! Yep, it's coo'. Two can play these fucking kid games." I was now talking to myself more than I was talking to him but oh well, at least he heard me and I was getting it all off my chest now.

"Erin, you got me fucked up! You better not try no dumb shit and get you and whatever nigga fucked up playing with me. If I find out, you fucking another nigga while you pregnant with my seed I'm going to dead both of yawl and I put that shit on my mom's grave. Yeah, you didn't think I knew your sneaky ass was in Planned Parenthood the other day, now did you? Your snake ass sister is the one who told me. So why were you there? Why you ain't tell me you had an appointment? You act like I ain't realized the change in your appetite and attitude lately. I know you pregnant but the question is what were you there for? Was you going to find out about the pregnancy or were you going to get an abortion? Shit, is that it? Is that why you want to keep arguing and accusing me of some shit because you trying to get rid of the pregnancy because you did some shit and it might not be mine? You wanted to talk and argue about some shit, so talk! Answer my fucking questions, Erin!" I couldn't believe he had just confronted me with that pregnancy shit. I didn't know he knew anything about it. I did see Kena's car, but I didn't see her or my sister, so I assumed Kena was there getting some meds for her sick ass pussy. Had I known them bitches were there watching me and waiting to report to Dame I would've talked to him about it first. Shit, I had just found out two days ago I was pregnant again. I mean I planned on telling him, but after I found out if he was back fucking his baby mom or not. How do you tell a nigga you're pregnant when he's already dealing with one baby mom who is off her rocker and causing y'alls relationship to be strained? No, I didn't want to have another abortion, but there was no way I was about to bring a child into this world with this back and forth shit with Kena.

"Yeah, that's exactly what the fuck I thought. Your stupid ass over there speechless. Ain't got nothing to say now, do you? You so worried about what the fuck my baby mom putting on Facebook and Twitter that you're not even keeping up with what needs to be worried about between us. Fuck this shit. I'm not about to sit here and argue with your simple ass all night. I'm out. You can sit here and think about the dumb shit all night by your damn self for all I care," Dame said as he hopped out of bed and threw on a pair of sweatpants to leave out. I didn't want this conversation to go this way, but now everything was out and on the table. I would have rather talked to him about our situation with my pregnancy at a different time and not in the middle of an argument about his baby mom, but that's what happened. I guess that's what happens when you try to address some shit without making sure your ass was in the clear first. I'm not in the business of kissing nobody's ass so I allowed Dame to leave without protesting for him to stay. If he wanted to run away from our problems like a little ass boy, then that was his problem, not mine.

Dame and I have been at odds ever since that night he stormed out of my apartment. Other than seeing him every day around the shop, I hadn't seen much of him. Dame would stop by my apartment here and there to grab something of his or to drop off money for me, but that was it. Our communication was even short. He texted me asking me to schedule an appointment for my pregnancy and let him know the details, but the "good morning" or simple "What you doing" texts stopped. Like I said, I wasn't going to kiss his ass so I let his ass be. Dame made a few little sly remarks about who I was with or what I was doing when he did say something to me. I could tell he had lost some of the trust in me he once had. I'll be the first to admit that it hurt my feelings being accused of fucking with someone else. The last thing I wanted was for Dame to think I was out fucking around on him because I wasn't. Since the first time Dame and I had sex I haven't fucked anyone else. Shit, there was no reason for me to cheat since we fucked more than porn stars and my needs were always fulfilled.

Today is my first real appointment with an OBGYN, outside of that little appointment I had at Planned Parenthood, and Dame was meeting me here. I didn't know what to say to him or how to even act around him with the strain we had between us right now. As bad as I missed being with him every night, I refused to play his doormat or sit back and watch him do me wrong. As soon as the nurse came out to call me back, Dame was walking in the door. He followed behind the nurse and me toward the room she placed us in so we could wait for the doctor. I had already given a urine sample when I signed in as well as filled out all of the necessary paperwork, so the majority of what I came here for was done. The doctor was only going to confirm I was pregnant, tell me a due date, as well as prescribe some prenatal vitamins. I was hoping to be lucky enough to get an ultrasound to see the little seed growing inside of me or at least hear the heartbeat.

"Why you sitting over there acting all timid and shit?" Dame asked.

"I'm not, why you say that?"

"Cause you real quiet. Normally you got a mouthful to say about any and everything," he said in a joking tone. As soon as I was ready to respond, the doctor walked into the room with a clipboard in hand.

"Hello, Mommy and Daddy to be! I'm Dr. Christian." The doctor reached out to shake both of our hands with a smile on her face.

"Hello, Dr. Christian," Dame and I both said in unison.

"Well let me start off by congratulating you both on the pregnancy. Today will go by pretty quickly; I only have a few questions to ask based on your paperwork. I will also give you guys the projected due date along with a prescription for some prenatal vitamins I will need you to take daily."

"So we ain't goin' to get to see the baby on the screen over there today?" Dame asked.

"I'm sorry, based off of the information Erin provided us with on her missed period, she is only eight weeks today and there honestly isn't much for you to see just yet. What I can do for you today is allow you to hear your baby's heartbeat. That's the next best thing I can offer. By the time of the next appointment, we can do an ultrasound so you guys can see."

"Ok, that's fine! Something is better than nothing," I replied.

"So, Erin, going over your paperwork briefly I see you don't have any major health concerns or conditions, which is great news. I see here that it states this isn't your first pregnancy within the past year. I have to ask you this so that we are making sure we ensure that you have the healthiest pregnancy possible. Did you miscarry the last pregnancy or terminate it?" Hearing the question escape her lips caused my breath to leave my body. Had I known those types of questions would come up, I would have asked her to discuss them with me personally, without Dame in the room. I had yet to tell Dame about my abortion and from the confused look on his face, I knew I had some serious explaining to do.

"I...I terminated that pregnancy," I said in a low tone, full of embarrassment.

"You what? When was this?" Dame's voice was loud enough for those to hear in the waiting room. He was more than heated and it was no secret.

"I'm sorry, sir, I'm going to have to ask you to lower your tone some for the privacy of our patients. However, Erin, I will need to know the date of the procedure. Knowing the details will allow us to determine if you were completely healed prior to becoming pregnant again," the doctor explained.

"I believe it was either eight or nine months ago," I responded without ever looking up to see the look on Dame's face.

"Oh, is that right?" Dame responded in a sarcastic tone. I was now regretting him being here for my initial appointment.

"Ok, Erin. Normally that is more than enough time to heal properly and carry a child without any complications. We will still keep a close watch on you because of this. Now that we have those questions out of the way, let me grab my baby Doppler so you guys can hear your little one's heartbeat," the doctor said while grabbing an instrument connected to the computer that looked like a small microphone with a flat surface. I laid back on the table I was sitting on and raised my shirt. When she started rubbing the microphone looking thing on my stomach, at first it only sounded like a bunch of water swishing around, then I heard a loud, strong, and rapid heartbeat. The sound of my child's heartbeat brought tears to my eyes that I wasn't expecting. The mood I was feeling prior had drifted away. I was now overjoyed and nothing else mattered. I know I fucked up by killing my first child but I promised not only myself, but God and this child that I will do everything in my power to love, protect, and be here for my baby. I looked over at Dame and he now had a smile on his face as well. I saw him blink a few times and it appeared as if he was holding back tears as well. I'm guessing the sounds of our baby's heartbeat warmed his heart as well and changed the mood he was in.

After my appointment, I headed home to prepare me something to eat. I may not be that far along but that doesn't mean I haven't already started craving every freaking thing. It's like I wanted to eat all the time and nothing was ever filling enough. One thing I am thankful for is that unlike Renee, I'm able to keep down all of my food; I haven't thrown up one time. If this baby is anything like its parents, it's going to be a little porker for sure. Dame texted me shortly after my appointment letting me know he would be over here within the next hour so we could have a talk. He made sure to make it clear he was coming to talk to me and not argue. I'm glad he was being the bigger person because I didn't know how to address our problems at this point. As soon as I finished making my chicken salad sandwich and sat on the couch, the front door was being opened. Dame walked in with bags from Babies 'R' Us, causing me to smile. He must have gone straight there after the appointment and got carried away. It was still early so we couldn't even see the baby on the ultrasound and this fool was already out buying baby stuff. We wouldn't be able to find out the sex for a while, so I hoped everything he purchased was neutral or it would be going right back to get exchanged. It's cute to see Dame being a happy and proud father without it having to be forced on him. No matter how upset Dame made me over this short period of time we've been "beefin'", that's still my baby and I can't lie and say I don't miss him and us being happy.

"Look, Erin, I'm going to get straight to the point with you and I'm not sugarcoating shit for you, ma. I'm salty as fuck you got an abortion without telling me. If my calculation is correct we were fucking around nine months ago, meaning the baby you killed was my fucking seed. I know it's your body and ultimately up to you whether you carry a baby or not, but you could've at least talked to me about it. You didn't even care how I felt about it. That shit hurt. Then to think that you didn't even tell me about this pregnancy either only makes me wonder were you planning on doing the same shit if I would have never brought it up. That right there ma is some low-down sneaky shit and I can't get with that sneaky bullshit. I'm not rocking with no chick I can't trust and right now you got me questioning if I can trust you or not. Now you're carrying my seed now... I mean, that is my seed, isn't it?" Dame asked with raised eyebrows like he needed some sort of confirmation.

"Yeah, of course, it's your baby," I replied innocently.

"Ok then coo'. From this point on, whatever has to do with your pregnancy or my seed, I want to be included. I didn't have the opportunity to be there for Lil Dame and I'm not trying to go through that shit again. For the sake of a smooth, stress-free pregnancy and our relationship, I'm going to let go of the fact you hid that abortion from me. But I will promise you this, the next time you go do some serious shit like that without at least talking to, I'm going to fuck your sneaky ass up. You hear me?"

"Yes, Dame, I hear you. I'm sorry I didn't talk to you about it. I just assumed that since we were just talking at the time and fresh that you wouldn't want a baby by me, considering you already had one baby mom as a headache. I didn't want to add to the massive amount of stress you already had. I promise you I will include you in any and everything that has to do with our child from this point on."

"Ok, ma, now get up and take them clothes off; daddy missed that pussy," Dame said while dropping the remaining bags he still had in his hands and removing his shirt.

"Dang, babe, I can't even see what you got the baby first?" I asked, laughing while standing to my feet to walk towards him.

"Hell naw, it's been too long and I need to be inside of you right now. Shit, my dick dry as fuck and I know what you got can fix my problem. You can look through this shit when we done." Dame's aggressive demeanor and sexy ass were causing my pussy to cream at just the thought of feeling him inside of me. Needless to say, I started undressing right there, forgetting all about my chicken salad sandwich.

ZION

Yawl heard enough about me from the mouth of others, now it's time for yawl to get to know me personally. I'm Zion, but you may hear Lee refer to me as Z, which is my nickname I was given as a youngin'. If you ask me, I would like to say I'm a pretty handsome nigga. I stand six feet tall, weighing two hundred and twenty pounds. I have a muscular build from years of little league basketball and football. I rock my hair in neatly twisted dreads and have the bad boy persona, but I'm a good dude for real. I was born and raised in the dirty south so I have that southern hospitality personality. Born in Jackson, Mississippi and raised in Atlanta, Georgia; I'm a certified down south breed. I'm the oldest of five and grew up in a single-parent household. There are three boys, including myself, and two girls. I'm the oldest, but my siblings and I are all legit nine months apart. It's like as soon as my mom had one, she was knocked up with another. My pops walked away from my mom after my youngest sister was born. My mom never really gave us an excuse or reason for my father's disappearing act, but if you ask me, no excuse was good enough, so I couldn't care less. Momma did her damn thing raising five kids on her own with help from my grandma, so as soon as I got the feeling of the street life and fast money, I took it upon myself to get out there and get it. The motivation behind my hustle was to not have to sit back and watch my momma work her ass off day in and day out at some rich assholes company, making him even richer while they only pay her petty change. Since I hopped off the porch I haven't turned back. I started off just nickel and dime hustling, but I'm proud to say I worked my way up the food chain and now a nigga eating good and my mom's ain't got to work for nobody unless it's her choice to do so out of boredom. Now I'm not saying I'm a millionaire or some shit, but let's just say I'm living comfortably.

I make trips to Ohio on a frequent basis to visit my grandma. My mom's mother moved up here a couple of years back when she retired, and just recently got sick. She's been in and out of the hospital for about six months. The doctors diagnosed her with Paget's disease, which was a surprise to hear. With my grandma being from down south, she always seemed healthy or had a remedy to heal whatever the problem was. She started off complaining about bad pains in her bones and lower parts of her legs all the time, then she started having trouble walking and severe migraines that wouldn't go away. After months of complaints and the symptoms getting worse, she finally decided to go see a doctor and we discovered her illness. They say she's had this for quite some time but with her getting older and no longer working as much, it's just starting to affect her. Some days are better than others and some days are pretty bad for her. I try to come visit her as often as I can in fear that her days may either be numbered or the next time I come she may no longer be able to walk. My grandma has always been a busy woman and to sit around without her mobility is going to send her to an earlier grave than anyone would have projected for her. During one of my frequent hospital visits to see my grandma, I ran into Lee. Well, she ran into me, literally, and we been in contact since that day.

The day I met Lee she was in a wheelchair and looked as if she had been through some sort of freak accident, but that didn't hide her natural beauty. The moment I laid eyes on her I gave her the nickname "Amoy". Amoy means beautiful goddess, and that's exactly what Lee is. Lee reminded me so much of the rapper Dej Loaf and that was, in my opinion, one of the coldest females walking this earth, so I was automatically attracted to her. After getting to know Lee and having several conversations, I discovered not only was she a beautiful woman, but she was very intelligent. It's hard to find a woman so young with a good head on her shoulders these days. It's like all women want to do is pretend to be the next celebrity and find a man to take care of them. Lee didn't send me any of those types of vibes. We talk on a daily basis, but whenever I'm in Ohio I make sure to go kick it with her. The first few months of knowing her she was still in the recovery stages so I would only come visit her over her parents' house and chit chat with her but lately, we've been kicking it pretty hard. I try to take her out and show her a good time whenever I'm around because other than work and school, that girl does nothing. I actually like the fact that she doesn't do much because I was never attracted to the type of women that were always in the streets doing God knows what. Lee is nine years younger than me but she is very mature for her age, so the age doesn't bother me any.

I like wining and dining Lee because I see potential in her. I can see myself settling down and trying something serious with her in the long run. Never being in a serious relationship before, I can see one coming in the near future. I'm damn near thirty and I ain't trying to grow old alone. I don't want to rush anything and she has admitted that she isn't ready for anything serious either, so we are on the same level. Before I try to get into anything serious I have to make sure I'm good financially and well off enough to leave the streets alone. When I do settle down, I don't want to be the type of nigga that has to juggle my home life and the streets; that's when problems surface. When the time to step back and live the real grown man life comes, I plan on having some babies and running the street ain't the type of example I'm trying to set for my offspring. I have a couple of businesses that I own and operate in Atlanta, so my money flow won't be affected by me stepping away from the game. I'm no dumb nigga, so all these years of hustling wouldn't be in vain.

I believe some shit Lee went through in her last relationship fucked her up bad because she has a guard up that I see slowly coming down. It took us months to even kiss, so the night I got some pussy I was in shock. Lee was tighter than a muthafucka so that let me know she wasn't out here just poppin' her pussy for everybody. I had to let her know from the moment I stuck my dick inside of her if she was fucking with someone else or even thinking about it that shit was a wrap. Plus, I ran into Lee raw our first night. It wasn't intentional but we were both in the moment so shit just played out that way. I may not be trying to settle down right now, but I'm not the type of nigga who runs around fucking multiple bitches at a time. I have too much respect for women to operate like that. Being raised by women, certain shit the average nigga might do I just can't get down with.

Being from down south and coming up to Ohio on the regular really shows me exactly why I will forever remain a down south nigga. Don't get me wrong, the women up north are finer than a bitch, but the niggas up north are truly a bunch of characters I can't see myself surrounding myself with. When Lee and I were out on one of our many dates, we ran across her ex-nigga. When I say this dude is a true definition of a clown ass, that's exactly what I mean. I had to check the nigga real quick because of the way he approached Lee. It didn't help that I could sense some uneasiness from his presence. I didn't want to have to body dude but if he continued with the disrespect in my presence I would have to take matters into my own hands. It was bad enough he felt the need to come approach her while we were out together, but to come at her in an aggressive ass way pissed me off. The nigga backed off once I said a few words to him, but I could tell from his boldness that it wouldn't be the end of him. He may never approach her again while with me, but he is for sure going to continue to try with her. You can always tell when a nigga ain't over or let go of a female just by the way he reacts to her presence. Lee assured me she was in the process of avoiding him no matter how hard he reached out to her, but she never explained why. There was no pressure for her to tell me why she cut dude off or was so adamant about not fucking with him because I wasn't concerned about her past. What happened before me is just that, before me. I'm in her present and will be in her future and that's all I care about.

My sister still hadn't completely forgiven me for dealing with Lee. She swears I knew about Lee's ties to Mark all along and I was just too selfish to care. In all honesty, I didn't know. I had only met Mark through my sister, so how in the hell was I supposed to know that he knew Lee or had history with her sister, Renee. My sister is my heart. We have always shared a close bond growing up and anything I can do for her to make her happy, I've always been willing. Nyla wanted me to cut all ties with Lee but that's the exact way I had begun to feel about my nephew's father, Mark. In my opinion, he was a sorry excuse for a man. He doesn't have a real job with any type of 401k to fall back on for the sake of my sister or their son, yet he still feels comfortable enough to sit around and chill at my sister's place every day. Up until I purchased a loft downtown when Lee got into her car accident, I had been funding my sister's living expenses with the help of my parents, but that luxury was about to come to an end. I have no problem helping my sister or my nephew out, but I refuse to be paying bills for another grown man to lay around on his balls. Nyla knows I'm a little fed up with the lack of drive and effort Mark puts in so she's been keeping her distance. I don't know what Mark has done to my sister, but he has her love struck! Nyla was never a weak female, so I only hope that Mark treats her damn good outside of not being able to financially support her. A part of me found that hard to believe though because of the comment Lee made about Nyla being Mark's side piece originally. I'm trying my hardest to stay out of her relationship because she is a grown woman and has a family of her own now, but I find it hard to when she's so dependent on me.

Roi'al was born a month early which was pretty scary for my family, but we are all thankful he is healthy. There was no real reason given for him being born prematurely, but something tells me my sister wasn't following doctors' orders about taking things easy. She had recently moved back in with my parents until her new place was finished being remodeled. I was happy that she chose to move into a bigger place further in the suburbs because she now had a son to raise and the place she had wasn't big enough for both of them. Our family had spoiled him so much he needed two rooms just for his own belongings. I've been in Columbus since my nephew was born because I fell in love with him at first sight. Being around him all the time made me have baby fever, but since I had yet to settle down, that wasn't in the near future. I'm ready to settle down and be a family man, but the only person I really want is Lee. She still has me stuck in this friend zone but has promoted me to best friend. I was cool with us only being friends originally, but I just knew she would eventually see me as having the potential to be more over time, but that never happened. Even after her back to back situations with Coby and my supportive shoulder to lean on, she was still resistant.

Lee shared so many personal things with me that there wasn't a fact about her I didn't know. From her favorite color being black to her weird fear of spider webs. Her family loves me and accepts me, which is a plus. On several occasions, I've confessed my true feelings about her, but she always brushes it off as me being drunk. Granted, I do always wait until after I've had a couple drinks or two to profess my love for her, but that's the only time I have enough courage. It's hard opening up to someone and trying to lay your feelings on the line when you're being rejected. Rejection is a bitch and no one likes to continuously experience it from the same person. I can truthfully say I love Lee, better yet, I'm in love with her and I just wish she would see it. Making matters worse, she's recently been spending time with some hoodlum from Atlanta she met while in the hospital. She tells me all about their little dates and time spent, which only hurts, but I brush it off while talking to her as if it doesn't bother me. I can tell that she has started to like the guy from the twinkle she has in her eye whenever she talks about him. I wish she had the same twinkle in her eye when it came to me, but I see I'm going to have to prove to her that I'm better for her than this nigga as well. Sitting in the corner having another cup of jungle juice at one of the frat parties on OSU campus with my frat brothers from Ohio, I could only think about Lee and what she was doing or who she was with.

ME: Wyd?

Lee: Nothing much! Wyd?

ME: Chillin' with my bros.

Lee: Sounds eventful. Make sure you don't get too wasted. LOL

ME: I'm not, I got to keep Roi'al in the morning for my sister.

Lee: That's what's up!

Me: Wya?

Lee: On my way downtown with Zion.

ME: It's late to be just heading downtown isn't it?

Lee: Yeah but we are going to walk on the riverfront and talk.

ME: I can't believe you are really getting serious with that thug.

ME: Well enjoy your night.

ME: I guess you're too busy all of a sudden to reply so I'll just talk to you tomorrow.

Me: Be careful.

After my comment about her little friend being a thug, she stopped replying to my text messages. I knew she read them because with iPhones it shows when the receiver opens a message; it says read. Her not replying only grinded my gears, causing me to get another cup of jungle juice and finish the bottle of Jack Daniels off. Getting drunk wouldn't help the situation or my feelings any, but it would make it easier to cope with something that was completely out of my control.

Lee and I hadn't talked much over the last few days and as hard as it is, I've been trying not to blow her up or reach out. I want to give her some space, but I fear that will only allow her new found friend to get closer to her so I can't. Today I sent two dozen flowers to her parents' house with a gift card to her favorite store, Buckle, with hope she would reach out to me after receiving her surprise gifts. I know money can't buy you love but I needed something to get her attention. We went from conversing daily and having lunch dates whenever I was in Columbus, to barely talking and text messaging being our primary form of communication. Any woman in their right mind would be throwing themselves at my feet if I gave them the time of day that I give Lee. Not to mention, I basically put my life on hold to be by her side when she went through her accident and recovery, all for her to move on with the next guy like I hadn't been waiting patiently for my turn to love her the right way. She's not going to do anything besides end up hurt again and looking stupid. Once this next clown, Zion, breaks her heart like Coby did, I'll be right there to fix the pieces and mend it, but the next time around I'm claiming what's mine in the process.

On top of my stress with Lee, my parents have decided to stop funding my sister, practically disowning her. My father explained that Mark had gotten himself into some type of trouble that he was unsure about. When my parents gave Nyla the ultimatum of leaving him alone or being cut off, she chose her son's father over her family. My parents just knew with Nyla not having any source of income and needing to take care of Roi'al she would choose her family, but she didn't. They say love will make you do some stupid things, but that had to be by far the dumbest thing Nyla could've done. Since the situation had nothing to do with me and Nyla was still my sister, I chose to step in and help her as badly as I didn't want to for the sake of my nephew. Family is everything to me and I can't see myself just turning my back completely on my own blood, no matter how unhappy I am with their choices or relationships. As bad as I needed to stay in West Virginia, I had no other choice but to move up to Ohio. It would be less expensive than commuting on a weekly basis, on top of taking care of two households. It would have been easier to just move us all into one big house and let go of my loft, but in no way could I stay under the same roof as Mark. Not only was he a lazy ass excuse for a man still, but he now had trouble coming his way. I need to have a safe haven for Nyla to go in case of an emergency. While finishing up packing the last few items in my closet, I heard my phone going off. I wanted to allow the caller to go to voicemail so I could finish up this packing, but I was glad I didn't when I saw Lee's name scroll across the home screen of my phone.

"What's up, Lee?" I greeted her.

"Hey, Best Friend! How are you?" She sounded like she was in a good mood and that made me smile until I thought about Zion being the cause of it.

"I'm good, other than being tired. How are you, miss lady?"

"I'm great, thanks for asking. I meant to call you sooner and tell you thanks for the beautiful flowers and my gift card. That was so random and I was super geeked to have a surprise waiting for me after a long day. Between work and school, I be super tired."

"You're welcome. I'm glad I could bring a smile to your face from a surprise. There are plenty more where that came from, but you know that already."

"Rod, you do not have to buy me things. I cherish our friendship for many other reasons and you know that," she replied, once again throwing that friend bullshit up in my face.

"Here you go, Lee. If I want to spoil you then allow me to."

"Whatever you say, Rod! Hold on, my line is beeping. Hey, Rod, this is Zion calling. If I don't call you back tonight, I'll hit you up tomorrow after my noon class."

"Yeah, ok, that's what you always say, but I'll be in Columbus tomorrow so I'm going to drop by campus so we can do lunch, so make sure you're available."

"Ok coo', bye!" Lee said, rushing to click over to her incoming call.

Moving from state to state and two separate houses wore me completely out, but I couldn't allow that to stop me from seeing Lee today. I had to cancel our lunch date because Mark was dragging his ass moving this morning, so it took us longer than I expected to finish moving everything. It worked out to my advantage though because Lee said she was off tomorrow and didn't have any classes, so I planned on taking her out and having a couple of drinks. Hopefully, she would be willing to stay at my loft with me tonight and finish off our night together. Now living in Columbus, I planned on making Lee mine. All I need is a few months to show her how devoted I am to her and that there isn't a better man for her than me.

I love the streets, I'm a gangster, I like to be in them daily
Your mother love me like a son but I'm not seein' me changing
A lot of built up frustration due to past situations
I ain't too hard to tell you how I feel
When you tat my name on it make me know it's real
I ain't too hard to tell you how I feel
What you say you don't do, you know I will

Kevin Gates' "Ain't too hard" filled the speakers in my car as I rode to Coby's apartment. Ever since Zion got me hip to this song I had it on repeat. I swear that nigga Kevin Gates is the truth and he could get it. Not being a groupie or anything, but he is finer than aged wine. I turned my phone off whenever I went to see Coby just because I didn't want to have to explain to anyone where I was or why I was even around him. Since I was waiting on my supervisor to return my call about my request to be off, I had to leave it on. Placing my phone in my back pocket, I headed up the steps to Coby's apartment. Yeah, the same one I ran out of the night that nigga kicked my ass for his own infidelities.

I still can't believe I allowed Coby's mother to convince me to talk to him, let alone come check on him. This was the third time in less than two weeks that I had come to his place to just check on him and spend a little bit of time with him. When Coby's mom first called I thought she was just calling to check on me, but when she told me that Coby had been going through something and was recently in and out of the hospital for some outrageous behaviors and outburst, I felt bad. There is still a soft spot in my heart for him for some reason, even after all we've been through. I felt an obligation to be there for him in his time of need because of the love we once shared. Coby was diagnosed with paranoid schizophrenia, which explains why he would randomly have a change in mood and get extremely jealous or feel like I was his possession instead of a girlfriend. His mom tried to explain to me that the medicine he was prescribed, mixed with recreational drug usage was the cause of the sudden violent spells he started having. I'm not giving him any excuse, but it all made sense to me because Coby wasn't like that in the beginning of our relationship.

The past two times that I've come to visit with Coby things seemed to be back to normal with his behavior. He was super nice and caring like he was in the beginning of our relationship. He had even apologized for everything he had done to me and I felt like it was sincere. His driving privileges had been revoked because of an episode he had one night on campus, so whenever I came over, he always wanted to go somewhere and up until today, I wasn't up for it. Today was a nice fall day to go feed the ducks, so I finally took him up on his offer of getting out of his apartment and going to Hoover Dam. Like I said, his driving privileges were revoked so we took my car. Coby was observing the scenery as we rode like he hadn't been outside of his apartment in ages. I didn't know if it was his medicine that was causing him to zone out the way he did or the fact that he had really been cooped up in his apartment since his parents finding out about his lifestyle changes, on top of his illness.

We ran out of bread within the first ten minutes of being at the park due to the number of ducks that surrounded us when we started feeding them. I wanted to just sit down and enjoy the peace of mind and nature, but Coby wanted to take a walk on the trail. I agreed only on the strength that there would be no telling when the next outing he would have would come and I understood the frustrations of being stuck indoors when everyone is trying to protect you all too well.

"Lee, do you ever think about us?" Coby randomly asked and his question caught me by surprise because we had been walking in silence since we started on the trail.

"What do you mean when you say us?" I asked for more clarification on the label "US".

"Like, do you think about the time we shared together and if we will ever be again?"

"Coby, you my first everything, including love, so there are many things I shared with you that I hold dear to my heart. Of course, I think about the times we shared and the relationship we had but as far as..." I was cut off by my ringing phone and I rushed to answer it without looking at the caller ID, in hopes of it being my supervisor finally returning my call.

"Hello?"

"I miss you, Amoy!" Zion's voice filled my ears and caused a smile to spread across my face.

"I miss you too, love," I said, without even thinking about Coby standing right beside me.

"How much do you really miss me? You miss me enough to come see me in the morning? I'll be at the hospital by like 9 to pick up my grandma. She was admitted yesterday, but she's just now telling me and they are discharging her tomorrow under close watch."

"I do, I do! Good thing I don't have any classes in the morning so that can be arranged."

"Coo', well let me get back to this count and I'll hit you up later."

"Ok, make sure you call me as soon as you're finished."

"I will. Send me a picture of them lips when we hang up since I can't get a kiss until tomorrow."

"Bae, you are a mess but I will when I get in the car. I'm out walking the trail right now."

"Alright, be careful."

"I sure will. Talk to you later." I ended the call and placed my phone back in my pocket, completely forgetting that Coby was right next to me the entire time. That's the effect Zion had on me. Whenever I heard his voice, was in his presence or even spoke his name, I was on cloud nine. The more time passed, I was finding it difficult to fight my feelings of being torn between wanting to take things to the next step with Zion or being single.

Whap, whap, whap! Coby smacked the shit out of me three times, back to back, in my face, bringing me right down to reality.

"You so fucking foul! You really just disrespected me without a second thought and carried on like we weren't just talking about us and our future. You're a stupid ass bitch." WHAP! Coby screamed at me and slapped me again. I was so caught off guard I couldn't do anything besides look at him in disbelief. He was really in the middle of Hoover Dam smacking me across my face like I was his punching bag.

"When I told you that if I couldn't have you no one would, I meant that shit, Lee! This relationship we have will never be over and the sooner you understand that the better off we will be." As I walked backward trying to get out of Coby's reach, he continued to walk toward me with hate in his eyes. How could a man that claimed to love you treat you the way he has and still think it's ok to be with them? When a person shows you who they are, you have to believe them, and I should've known that when he was medically diagnosed with paranoid schizophrenia aka crazy, that that's what and who he really was. Before Coby could back me completely against the bridge, I turned and ran as fast as I could to my car. Coby was no longer in the shape he used to be in while playing football, so he couldn't catch me. When I reached my car, I put my keys in the ignition and pulled off as fast as my car allowed me to go. I wasn't worried about leaving him in the middle of nowhere at Hoover Dam because if I hadn't, he could've beat my ass to a bloody pulp, or even worse, killed me. Picking up my phone, I dialed Coby's mother and of course, she didn't answer. I left her a voicemail to explain to her that I left her son because he once again put his hands on me and that she would need to either go pick him up or send the police to get him. Hopefully, they would admit him right back into the hospital because whatever they prescribed him obviously wasn't strong enough; he was a harm to others being a walking time bomb.

I can't believe this nigga really had the nerve to actually try me again. I put the past behind us and gave him another chance for us to actually be friends and he blew it. Aside from the fact that we could never actually be anything more, I thought we would work out just fine as friends, but I guess I was wrong once again. I felt bad for his stupid ass and allowed his manipulating ass mom to convince me to be there for him and it backfired on my ass. With all the talk about his illness, I had given him a pass and excused the previous things he had done, but fuck that. I'm sure she doesn't know the impact or severity of his actions on others. All she's thinking about is her son and I don't have time to be in this abusive ass lifestyle. There is no way in hell I'm about to sit around and be Coby's punching bag; I know I said that the last time. I also said the stunt he pulled when I walked in on him was the final straw, but I allowed his situation to make me feel bad and bring me back into his life. We are nothing more than just friends, so what would even allow him to think he has the right to control who I talk to or if I move on with my life or not. I pay the phone bill on my phone and it's my life so I'm the only one who has control of it and that is what Coby fails to realize. We aren't together and haven't been in months so for him to believe that I was going to remain single for the rest of my life is ridiculous. I could have walked away and talked on my phone, but that would have been rude too so, either way, I would've been in the wrong in his eyes. As bad as I wanted to fuck him up, I wasn't strong enough to fight Coby off in the middle of nowhere without any weapons. I want to call my brother and tell him but instead, I'm just going to walk away from Coby and his madness for good. It's cool though. I'm not going to trip or stress it because there isn't any proof of him hitting me besides being emotionally hurt. Karma is going to get Coby and eat his sorry ass alive. That's the best revenge I can have against him.

DUPREE

I heard Renee talking on the phone with Lee about that nigga Coby and if I'm not mistaken, she said that he had hit her again. When I heard *again*, I was in shock because Lee has never been the type to accept any type of fuck shit from anybody. Lee is a firecracker and ready to fight whoever, whenever, so this is a surprise to me. I didn't want Renee to think I was eavesdropping so I didn't bring it up to her. Besides, that's Lee's business so I don't want to overstep my boundaries. Then again, Lee is like a little sister to me and I can't sit back knowing some nigga is disrespecting her, or even worse, putting his hands on her. Lee's been through enough. She doesn't need to be going through no unnecessary headache, heartache or pain from no nigga. As far as we all knew, Coby and she were done and had been since she moved back, but I guess they must have worked through their issues and kept their relationship a secret. As far as we all knew, Lee had been kicking it with some new cat who wasn't from around here by the name of Zion. I made a mental note to talk to Kris about all this shit. Not for the sake of being in Lee's business, but for her own protection. If she wasn't able to protect herself, that's where Kris, Dame and I came in at; we were her brothers and whatever nigga she couldn't handle, we could.

On another note, it had been almost two months since Alisha gave birth to her son and I had yet to hear the DNA results. I'm no expert in this field but I know good and damn well I should've heard something by now. The phone number that I was able to reach her on previously was now disconnected, and whenever she called me it was always from a blocked number. She called at least twice a week just to converse; it was never about the baby. Whenever I would bring the baby up to get her focused on the matter that was more important, she would all of a sudden need to get off the phone. Alisha claimed that her phone was disconnected and that she wasn't able to pay the bill at the moment so she called whenever she was around someone who had a phone. Her reason for calling private was because she said she didn't want me calling back from random people's phones looking for her, which was bullshit if you ask me. Alisha was probably hoping I would offer her some money out of pity on the strength that her son could possibly be mine, but she was under false hopes if she thought I was giving her a dime before reading the DNA results. I won't lie, if the test comes back and proves that the little boy is mine I'm going to feel a little bad, just because since he's been discharged from the hospital I haven't seen him not one time. I feared getting attached and he belongs to the next nigga so to prevent causing myself any grief, I kept my distance.

Renee's baby shower is today and I'm starting to believe that I'm more excited than she is about this one. Not only is it a baby shower, but Renee will also be revealing the sex of our baby at the baby shower. No one knows the sex of the baby other than Renee, so it's going to be a surprise and shock to everyone there. I too have a surprise for Renee and I can't wait to see the look on her face when my surprise is announced. I really want a boy, but it'll be just my luck we will be having another girl. Lord knows I need some more testosterone in our household. Between Renee's pregnancy mood swings and Sanai's diva attitude, I don't know who is worse.

The baby shower was beyond nice. Although I didn't like the colors Renee chose when she mentioned them to me, they actually came together really well. Teal, chocolate, gold, and mint green decorations were everywhere. Since no one knows the sex of the baby, all of the decorations that were personalized displayed a different sonogram picture of our mystery baby. Lee, Netia, and Erin did a good job decorating for Renee. They brought her dream baby shower to life without her help. They had balloon arches set up over the entrance, with a mixture of the colors, as well as over the area Renee and I would be sitting. The "Sweets" table was decorated with color coordinating cake pops, chocolate covered rice crispy treats on sticks with ribbons tied around them and a four tier cake decorated with all types of baby items made out of fondant icing. Since Renee's mom loved to cook she prepared all of the food and wouldn't have it any other way. I tried to convince her to have the event catered, but she cussed me out as if I offended her. Fried and baked chicken wings, mash potatoes, green beans, pasta salad, fruit salad and dinner rolls was a pretty plush menu for a baby shower. The punch fountain had a teal colored juice with gold lights surrounding the spouts the juice poured from. Our guests gifted far too many items for them to all fit on a table, so they designated an area of the room for gifts. We were blessed to not only be able to provide for our child on our own, but to also have a ton of others here supporting and showing love as well. Everything appeared perfect to me and Renee was satisfied with the turnout, including the games and picture booth that was set up.

Renee wanted to help out so bad fearing that things wouldn't turn out the way she wanted and her special day would be ruined, but she was by far too damn big to be helping set up anything. Nae is a perfectionist when it comes to certain things and I prayed today would turn out in her favor because if not, she would be an emotional rollercoaster. I couldn't imagine Renee being much help anyways; her stomach would knock over half the shit she put up if she did. If the doctors wouldn't have assured us there was only one baby in there I would be willing to bet my last dollar that Renee was carrying twins. The weird part was she threw up so much I don't know how she was able to gain a pound over this pregnancy. Since her stomach and hips were the only things to grow, I'm sure she'll snap back from this pregnancy just like she did after she had Sanai. Even if she didn't snap back to her small figure, I love my woman and her size would never turn me off from being attracted to her.

When it was time to cut the cake, Renee announced that the color of the inside of the cake would be the reveal of the sex of our baby. Renee handed me the knife and allowed me to do the honors. I was eager as hell to find out what my baby was carrying, so the slice that I cut was far from perfect. I almost destroyed the entire tower of cakes trying to see the color. The bright colored blue cake caused a smile to appear on my face. "YEAH BOY!" I screamed while hitting my chest with my fist. The crowd cheered and applauded for the announcement of our son. I turned to Renee and gave her the sloppiest wet kiss ever. She was cheesing so hard and excited to finally be able to let her secret out. I know it was eating at her, keeping it in this long.

"Are you happy now, baby? You have your princess and prince," Renee said, wiping the spit off the side of my lips from the sloppy kiss we had just shared.

"Hell yeah, I'm happy. I mean either way I would've been happy, as long as the baby comes out healthy. But having my princess, prince and queen completes me," I said, and I saw the water building up in Renee's eyes.

"Before we go any further I have an announcement of my own. I would like to have everyone's attention really quick." I turned to Renee and grabbed her hands inside of mine.

"Renee, I want to thank you for being the phenomenal woman, mother, sister, daughter, and girlfriend that you are. I couldn't have asked for a better woman to carry and raise my children with. I've been in love with you since before you ever knew, and my love continues to grow stronger for you each and every day we are together. I can't wait for our son to be born and we continue our journey together. When people say they have relationship goals and real love is what they want, I picture us and smile. I have everything a man could ever ask for here with me and it's all because of you. You and our children are my entire world and I wouldn't have it any other way, so what I'm saying to you is..." I dropped to my knee and pulled the Zale's jewelry store box from my right pocket. "Will you continue to be the woman you are and carry my last name forever more?" All the guests started screaming and cheering us on in awe. The tears that were previously built up in Renee's eyes were now a waterfall down her cheeks.

"Yess, baby! Oh my God. Yes, Dupree, I'll be more than happy to carry your last name." I placed the three carrot yellow diamond engagement ring on her ring finger of her left hand and stood to my feet. Wrapping my arms around Renee, I felt a sense of completement. Renee completes me and the fact that we will grow old together watching our children grow up and live a happy life makes everything we've ever gone through worth it.

Now that the baby reveal, shower, and engagement was over, the next thing we had to do was move into our new place before my Jr. gets here. Renee and I agreed on naming my son after me, no matter what the results of Alisha's child's DNA say. All fingers were pointing to the baby not being mine just based on the fact she hasn't told me anything yet and I hadn't received anything in the mail saying the baby is mine. If he does turn out to be mine, we will just have to figure out another name for him other than Jr. Knowing Alisha's sneaky ass, she would still try to name him after me to get under Renee's skin, but that would only be fucked up toward the child and confusing for him.

I allowed Renee to pick the house for us to purchase and agreed to pay for it. Renee is my soon to be wife and whatever house she picked, I knew would be the perfect match for our family. I trusted her enough to be satisfied with her choice. The house she chose was a five bedroom, three and a half bathroom, two story house, with a finished basement, three car garage, full backyard including a patio, deck, and a below the ground pool. The house was a pretty penny and cut a nigga's pockets deep, but that's what all those years of investing and hustling were for. Being completely out of the game, I planned on sitting back and enjoying my time as a family man. The next thing was getting Dame to get completely out of the game before it's too late so we could both watch our kids from this side of the barbed wire fence. Our house is something I can look at and say I worked hard for with my blood, sweat, tears, and I'm proud of it. The furniture was also something I let Renee pick. Of course, she did all the shopping online and would have interior decorators come and assist her with putting her touches on it so it wouldn't be too much for her. The only room of the house Renee wasn't allowed to decorate was my man cave in the basement; that area was strictly mine. Nae complained that my place looked like a bachelor pad and that's exactly how I would decorate my area. Little did Renee know I planned to have a stripper pole installed so she could perform a few tricks after having our son. Renee kept telling me that she was getting on birth control and I couldn't touch her for at least the six weeks instructed by the doctor in fear of getting pregnant again. The way I see things, we will soon be married and she could have as many kids as her body allowed. God doesn't make any mistakes and if it's meant for her to get pregnant again, then so be it. We will have more than enough room, so why not keep being fruitful. When I told Renee that she said I had the game all fucked up and she wanted to have our wedding a year from our engagement at the latest, so she refused to walk down the aisle pregnant or fat. My response was I can't make any promises other than I will marry her no matter how she looks. My heart beats for her heart, not her shape.

$$\cdots\cdots\cdots$$

DAME

$$\cdots\cdots\cdots$$

A nigga just can't get right. It seems like the closer Erin and I get, the more random bitches interfere with my mind. I haven't confessed to her just yet, but Erin has a nigga's heart, I'm just scared to commit one hundred percent. Erin is a bad bitch and can have any man she wants, so if a nigga comes along whose money is longer than mine or dick is bigger, what assures me she won't chuck up the deuces on a nigga? I mean Erin has never rubbed me as the gold digger type, but money makes bitches cum whether they admit it or not. If I was a broke nigga, there's no way in hell Erin would still be around after the shit I done put her through in such a short period of time. Daddy do put the dick on her nice, but shit, I know I ain't the only nigga in the world with an anaconda as a dick. The tongue lashes serve her well too, but shit I ain't the first or last nigga to be Grade A at eating the pussy. Thoughts like this are what makes it hard as hell to keep my dick in my pants. I keep telling myself by the time Erin has my seed I'm going be done fucking up, but each day we get closer, I try to push it back a little more, buying myself more time to do stupid shit. Erin's flaws are her perfections, so it's not what she does or doesn't have that makes me cheat, it's me and my fears that cause the tipping out on her. The only thing I can promise is that one day I will get this shit right; I just don't know when exactly.

I've stuck to my word when I said I wouldn't be fucking with Kena's ass ever again. Even on the nights she would tempt me and my dick would be ready to think for me, I had to remind myself that the condom could break and then what? Ain't no way in hell I'm trying to have my dick all lumped up from the shit I witnessed on her pussy. On top of fucking myself up, I could risk passing that shit to Erin and my unborn. I would never forgive myself if I gave my unborn child something like herpes because of my own selfish reasons. Erin's doctor told her at her first appointment and every appointment after that she was healthy as far as STDs were concerned and that's how it's going to continue to go. After the night I accidentally passed out over Kena's house and woke up to her trying to suck my dick, I cut her off completely. I had to literally beat her ass like a nigga on the streets. She has always been the type to fuck with me and take it when I wouldn't give it to her, but she crossed the line trying to take advantage of me in my son's bed. I was high as fuck when I went over to her house and I only went over there so late at night because she said my son wasn't feeling well, so I dropped off some medicine and ended up falling asleep with him while trying to put him to sleep. Not only was the stunt she pulled disrespectful to my son, but my dick as well. I know for a fact she has herpes on her pussy, but I was unsure of her mouth and I couldn't take any chances. I hopped up out of my sleep so fast and punched her square in her fucking face. I leaked her shit pretty bad and blacked out and whipped her ass. I felt low key bad for going so hard on her but the level of pissed she took me to, I couldn't calm down fast enough to stop myself.

When I went home that night, I had Kena's blood on my shirt so I had to tell Erin the situation and how it all went down. Erin's ass was livid and ready to fight and I had to calm her ass down before she took her pregnant ass over to Kena's house on that bullshit. I don't blame her, but I couldn't allow her to fight my other baby mom while pregnant with my unborn. Under different circumstances, I would have finally let her get in Kena's ass, but not now. That's too much of a risk to my baby. Erin did let me know that when she saw Kena she couldn't promise she wouldn't spit in her face. My only prayer was she wouldn't run into her until a few more months when my baby was here. The same night all that went down over Kena's, Dupree called me and told me that one of our little niggas had caught Mark slipping and shot him up. The nigga didn't die, fortunately, but he got his payback. The nigga was shot seven times so that was more than double what he had done to my brother. He was as fortunate as Dame to have been grazed or shots that went strength through. He had one bullet stuck in his knee, two in his ass, one that shattered his other knee and three in the back. I'm surprised he didn't die from all those shots to the back, but God was on that man's side. Word on the streets is that he was transported straight to jail after he was released from the hospital. I'm sure his broke ass didn't have any money for a lawyer to help fight the charges Renee filed on him, so he would be sitting his ass in there for some time. If the nigga was released, he would be worse off than in the jail, so his best bet was to sit in there and enjoy those three hots and a cot.

"Dame, get your ass up here, man. Your stupid ass baby mom ran up on Erin talking shit and they got to fighting with Lil Dame standing right here. We got the fight broken up but this stupid bitch refusing to leave and I don't need nobody calling the fucking police to our shop, making it hot."

"What? Man, I'm on my way there now. What the fuck?" I said, ending the call before he could say anything else. Getting my brother's call about my baby mom coming to my place of business starting drama was her first mistake, then to hear she had my son with her pissed me off. Putting the icing on the cake, she targeted Erin, knowing good and well she would've never tried that shit if Erin wasn't pregnant. I put the pedal to the metal in an attempt to get to my shop as fast as possible.

Pulling up to the shop, Kena's dumb ass was still outside making a scene in front of the shop, yelling and throwing a fucking tantrum. She is far too old to be doing things like this. What reason did she even have to be at my shop and furthermore, arguing with my woman? Seeing my son standing there crying his eyes out caused me to see red, with Kena being the target.

"Bitch, what the fuck is your problem? Out here acting a muthafuckin' fool in front of my son like he needs to be seeing this type of shit. Lil Dame, go over there and get in the car," I instructed my son to go get in my car and Kena snatched him by the arm, preventing him from moving any further.

"He ain't going no fucking where. He came here with his mom and he's leaving with his mom. I'm sick of you thinking you run something, Dame, with your ain't shit ass. Tell your fat ass bitch to come out here so she can catch these hands since she wants to sneak me. That bitch knew I was taking my earring out!" Kena yelled, making herself look even more stupid. From her comment, I knew Erin must have whooped her ass because no bitch who wins wants a rematch, especially with their child standing there screaming and crying.

"Man, bitch, give me my fucking son and take your simple ass on somewhere. You causing too much of a fucking scene and for what? Cause I don't want your thot ass or because you jealous of my girl? Huh?" I asked, snatching my son from her grip and picking him up to comfort him.

"Dame, give me my fucking son. I'm not going nowhere without my son. If you want me gone, that's fine! I don't want your ass and your little miss piggy ain't shit to be jealous of with her fat ass. Bet she wouldn't be trying to fight over your sorry ass if she knew you were sharing your dick with the whole community. Fuck she thought that shit belonged to her. Nah, that shit for everybody." Kena didn't know any of my dirt, or so I thought, so she was only saying shit so Erin could hear her and come after me. Before I could say anything else, I heard yelling coming from inside of the building.

"Aye, we gotta get Erin to the hospital. She's bleeding, dog," one of the workers yelled.

"She's bleeding? What you mean bleeding? From where?" I asked in a panicked tone.

"We don't know for sure but her pants have blood running down them like she's pissing blood or something, dog. We gotta hurry up, ain't she pregnant? That can't be a good sign," he said before heading back in the building to get Erin.

"Bitch, I swear to God on my mom's grave if something happens to my girl or my unborn child, I'm going to kill your thot ass and let Erin raise our son! Now take my fucking son and get the fuck out of here." I put my son back down and ran towards the building to help get Erin.

After three and a half hours of being at the hospital, making sure that everything was ok and checked out with Erin, we were finally home. I made sure the doctors ran all types of tests to prove my unborn wasn't harmed and ok. They promised us that the baby was fine and that Erin was just experiencing something called implantation bleeding. The doctors couldn't tell us if it was related to the previous abortion or something that could have happened today. They said it isn't common, but it can happen. Erin's blood pressure was also high, which I'm sure was a result of her getting all hyped up over fighting Kena. We didn't share the fact that Erin had been in a fight with the hospital or their staff because we didn't need a social worker involved or the police. Better believe I got in Erin's ass though about her fighting while pregnant and putting not only herself in danger, but my unborn as well. She justified her reason for fighting by saying Kena got in her face and she was only defending herself because she was unsure of Kena's next move. I knew that Erin just needed a reason to kick Kena's ass, so her excuse went in one ear and out of the other.

The shit with Erin bleeding scared a nigga straight I think. The possibility of her losing my child over some stupid fight my baby mom started with her opened my eyes. That could have been any of the females I gave the dick to trying to be spiteful and anything could've gone wrong. Since that day, I've been focused on Erin and the well-being of not only her and my unborn but our relationship as well. The shit is hard because of course my side pieces still hit my phone on the daily, but eventually they will catch the hint. If not, a nigga is going to have to change his number because fighting temptation is hard as fuck. Erin is now considered high risk so if it's not work, she's at home. I don't want her doing anything extra. I don't even want her helping me out around my office just because she doesn't have to or need to for the money. We contacted my attorney after the fight at my business to put a rush on the custody shit with Lil Dame. As of right now, with all the negativity surrounding Kena, the courts would be in favor of my son being placed with me, so I'm feeling real confident about the outcome once we receive our court date.

Is this what it's like to be in love? I find myself asking this question almost every day. The feeling I have that's caused by Zion is indescribable. We are so compatible it's impossible to continue to fight my feelings for him. We've not officially made things official but you might as well say we are a couple. Everyone already thinks we are together and we do everything like we are. When he refers to me he calls me his Amoy or his future wife, so I guess it's safe to say I'm his and he's mine. I'm happy I found Zion and got another chance at love after Coby because I was misled into believing that what Coby and I shared was love. Now I see what we shared was only lust and a mixture of the puppy love that I swore it wasn't. I haven't heard from Coby since the day at Hoover Dam and I'm not sure if me changing my number is the result of it or if he's back in the mental hospital. No matter the reason, I'm happy to not have to deal with his headache.

I've been doing a lot of traveling lately and spending time with Zion in his hometown. I've switched all my classes to online courses so I'm not falling behind and my studies are still doing well. My GPA for the most recent semester was a 3.8. No, it's not perfect, but college ain't no joke. Ohio State University seems so much harder than West Virginia State. I still work at the recreation center but only part time and I'm able to pick and choose which days I work. I had to slow down on work because it was interfering with not only my school work but my time to spend with bae. That sounds funny but it's the truth. I'm still all about my coins, but living with my parents all this time and never really having any bills of my own, I have been able to save up a nice amount of money. Zion doesn't allow me to pay for anything anyways so I'm good in the financial department. I'm starting to think it's time to move out of my parents' house anyhow. I want to move to Atlanta for a new start and fresh beginning with my new found lover. Zion suggested it a few weeks back and I told him I would think about it and give him an answer soon. After my talk with my parents and getting their blessing, my mind was made up. It's not like I wouldn't be home often. Zion's grandma still isn't doing well so he will continue to travel back to Ohio on a weekly or biweekly basis at the least.

Rod and I aren't close anymore. I hate that our relationship has changed because Rod and I were at one point extremely close, but he has become very jealous and territorial when it comes to Zion. It's like Rod doesn't want me around anyone if it isn't my family or him. I've told Rod time and time again how I feel about him and I've never once led him to believe that we would ever be more than friends. Rod still reaches out to me and tries to convince me of his strong feelings for me, but I've been trying to ignore him. I confessed and told him that I had sex with Zion and that fool damn near had a heart attack talking about how could I be so stupid and naive to fall for another one. When he referred to Zion as "another one", I was unsure of what he meant exactly, but little did Rod know, Zion and Coby were not one in the same. I don't feel like I have to explain nor go into details to show him all the ways Zion is right for me, so I let him believe what he wants to. What's understood doesn't need to be explained. For the sake of my own personal sanity, it's best I keep distance between Coby and me, as well as Rod and I.

Tonight is the night that I tell everyone about my upcoming choice to move to Atlanta. I also want to announce to everyone that I'm expecting. Getting pregnant while still in school was never in my plans, but neither was leaving Coby or finding love again so soon. I don't believe in abortions so that's not even an option. Zion and I haven't really talked much about kids besides the fact that we both don't have any and want some in the future. Well, in our case, the future has come sooner than later. I'm sure Zion's grandma will be overly excited because she keeps talking to Zion about giving her some great-grand-babies before she's too sick to enjoy them. My mom and dad I know will be in shock, but accepting, just because that's how they are. They never judge us or come down too hard on us for the decisions we make in our personal lives. Now don't get it twisted, I'm nervous about telling everyone, but tonight will be perfect because everyone will be in attendance. Breaking the news to everyone at once with all the good news and life changes we are all celebrating couldn't have been a better time to disclose the information I've been keeping. Renee is the only person I've told and that's because she went with me when I found out. Renee was like a big kid jumping around when we found out. She's due any day and I can't wait for my nephew to be born. I hope he comes before I move because I'm so anxious to meet him.

The family dinner turned into more of a big party at my parents' house. The entire family was there, even Aunt Gin's crazy ass. She kept asking Zion if he had an uncle or older brother for her. He laughed her off but her drunk ass was serious as fuck. Kris finally brought a woman home for everyone to meet, saying that he felt left out that all his niggas were now settling down and he was the only one running around single. We all knew she was just his flavor of the week but hoped he would make it something serious. The girl was cute and from what she told us, had her shit together. Being an RN at the age of 26 was a damn good accomplishment, especially with no kids or ex-husbands to trail behind her. Erin, Dupree, and Lil Dame came dressed alike, looking like a little family. I'm happy to see my girl pregnant on my bro's arm with a step son. Whether they are married or not, I say step son because Erin loves that little boy like he is her own and he loves her too. Renee, Sanai, and Dupree, of course, were in attendance and Renee was walking around looking like she was ready to give birth at any second. Dupree followed her around wherever she went like her shadow, scared she would go into labor soon. Sanai was growing up so fast and I swear with Rene being pregnant she was moving out the way because that little girl is grown as fuck. Netia came and said she had something she wanted to tell us as well. Seeing all my loved ones together and happy without stress and drama is a great feeling. Of course, I was so happy Zion came; it wouldn't be right if my special person wasn't in attendance for an event where I had an announcement to make. We have all been through a lot and deserve the happiness we are finally feeling. Over the last year so much has changed and looking at it now, it all happened for the better. We may not have known when we were going through our own personal storms why we were going through so much, but I'm a strong believer now that everything happens for a reason.

Each and every person stood and spoke on the good news that had been coming up in their personal lives and it was finally time for me to make my big announcement. My hands started sweating and I got butterflies when I stood and had everyone's attention.

"Well, they say you save the best for last and since I'm the best, here it goes," I joked to make it easier for me to break the news. "First and foremost, I want to tell everyone thank you and how much I appreciate the love and support yawl showed me over the last year. This has been one trying year and I'm happy to say, nigga, we made it." Everyone started laughing at me.

"Oh, get to the point already. Got us all over here sitting on the edge of our seat, chile," my aunt Gin interrupted, slurring.

"Ok, ok, ok. Well, first I want to say I have decided that I'm going to be moving out and moving to Atlanta with Zion. Before anyone says anything I'll be home..."

"I'm sorry, I can't allow that to happen!" I was once again interrupted but this time, it wasn't by my aunt Gin. The familiar voice caused the hairs on my back to stand. Not out of fear, but shock that he was in attendance. Rod had texted me earlier saying he needed to talk to me and I ignored his message because I wasn't trying to allow him to ruin my mood or day with his negativity or comments about anything going on in my life right now. I would tell him I'm moving once I was already moved so that way he couldn't throw another bitch fit or try to change my mind. With me not texting him back, I was never expecting him to pop up over my parents' house, unannounced or invited. Now that he was here, I could only imagine how things were about to go.

"Aww, shit! It's 'bout to go down in this bitch," Aunt Gin said. The looks on everyone's faces were shocked, pissed, confused and lost, including my own. *What is he doing here,* I thought to myself.

"Look, Lee, before you say another word, I've tried to reason with you and be patient, but I see it's not working. I've reached out to you only to get ignored and brushed off like I haven't been the perfect gentleman for you. I can't keep sitting back and watching you love everyone but me. I won't sit back and watch it happen. It's not fair. I see now how Coby felt. It's something about you that will cause the sanest man to go crazy about your love. I don't know how I allowed you to bring me to this point, but if I can't have you, neither will he." Rod raised his arm and I saw the chrome piece I hadn't realized until it was too late. I heard two loud shots fired along with screams, then I felt a burning sensation in my chest before collapsing to the ground.

"NOOOOOOO! She's pregnant yawl! Somebody call 911. Lee! Noooooooo!" Renee screamed.

It didn't matter what she said or did, I wasn't letting go and neither was she until I was ready. With the way I feel right now, I'll die before I see Lee walk away from me. I told Lee if I couldn't have her, neither would anyone else and I meant that. Since she felt like she was going to move and be with Zion, I had to do what I had to do. Unlike these other cats in Columbus, I don't fear her brother, his friends, nor her new boy toy, Zion. What they don't know is my money is long enough to buy me out of any situation. I don't fear anything, not even jail. If I did fear them niggas or even the system, I would've never done what I did. I can blame Lee for my sudden acts of craziness, but the truth is this has always been me. There was a reason I lived far away from my family and never talked much about them until recently. The things I did in my past, my parents couldn't handle, so it was best for me to be far away. Finally, I'm able to be free. Lee was the only woman I had ever loved or felt like I could be myself with and that's over, so why pretend to be someone I'm not? I know the life I live is shaky and I've caused a lot of hate towards me, but fuck it! I don't regret it. I'm thankful Lee showed me the truth before it was too late.

EPILOGUE

The day my son Dupree Jr. was born was one of the best, yet worst days of my life. Rod killed my sister. It's still hard to believe Lee is gone. Her life was taken far too soon. She was still so young and had so much life to live. Lee was too early on for them to save the baby, and I wish she would've been further so we would at least still have a piece of her left here on earth with us. All we have now are her memories. The two shots Rod fired into Lee's chest from a .22 bounced around, hitting all of her vital organs. There was no way she could have made it, even if the paramedics were on the scene when it happened. Someone called the police, but not before the guys of the family practically beat Rod to death. Luckily for him, no one was carrying their weapons because we were only expecting to have a great family gathering, and not a war in my parents' backyard.

My little family is doing well, other than missing Lee. My life will never be the same. My wedding is approaching soon and my sister won't even be there to be my maid of honor. Every day is hard. They say time heals all wounds but I'm not believing it. If it wasn't for my kids, I don't think I would have been able to push forward and continue to live my life. Sanai is growing so fast and is the best big sister to Jr. Jr. is a spitting image of his father and when I tell you he is more spoiled than Sanai was, I tell you no lie. Dupree makes every day easier for me with being the loving father and my soon to be husband. My parents moved shortly after Lee was killed. They both went back to work from their retirements and I believe that was the only way either of them knew how to handle what happened to their youngest child right in front of them. Kris went off the deep end and has been in the streets even more than before. We were all close, but Lee and Kris had a special bond that only they understood.

Erin and Dame are expecting their little girl. Dame was also awarded custody of his son, Lil Dame. Children Services were involved when a stranger found Lil Dame in the back of Kena's car one night while she was at the bar, getting drunk as always. I'm guessing the judge had had enough of giving her chance after chance and didn't even make Dame fight anymore. Netia moved back down south once she lost custody of Lil Dame. I guess she was too embarrassed to show her face around these parts anymore. Erin and Dame just recently moved into their first home together and it's the perfect size and fit for their little family.

Netia moved to New York and that was the news she shared with us that day of the killing. She is attending college and has finally found a significant other. Netia finally came out and admitted she has a girl-friend. We still keep in contact, but not as much as we used to because everyone has their own lives and little families to take care of. Netia promised to bring her girlfriend for all of us to meet before my wedding.

We ran into Alisha and her children at the mall one day. She tried to avoid us but it was impossible. The results from the DNA test taken were no longer needed when we laid eyes on her son. He looked just like her other child by her previous boyfriend. After seeing her in the mall that day she never called Dupree's phone ever again. She even apologized to him that day for causing the drama she had with her accusations. Nobody knows what happened to Ciara; aka Erin's big sister, when Kena disappeared Ciara did too.

Coby was never heard from anymore. Word around town was he lost the little sanity he had left when Lee was killed and is now a permanent resident of the Twin Valley Mental Hospital. Mark is still in jail facing seven years for a number of charges from the incident that took place at my apartment when he shot Dupree. Nyla is still around Columbus somewhere, raising her and Mark's son with the help of her parents. Rod, of course, was hospitalized after the beating he received from everyone following him shooting Lee, but he is currently awaiting trial for the murder of my sister.

Last, but surely not least, poor Zion. We were all devastated by the loss of Lee and their unborn child, but Zion took it pretty hard. Then to top it off, he lost his grandma the following week. I still keep in contact with Zion, but talking to him is hard. He breaks down at the end of every conversation feeling like he failed Lee by not being able to protect her from what happened. No matter how many times I try to convince him it wasn't his fault and there was nothing he could do about it, his personal guilt remains the same. I pray not only for my family daily but Zion as well. He deserves to find love and I know Lee would want him to be happy.

All in all, we went through some shit and when things turned around for us, we were hit with a ton of bricks. Finding love isn't always easy, but when you do, make sure it's right. You never know who's working with a few loose screws and can cause you to lose everything you have, maybe even your life. Love will make you do some crazy things, just make sure it's worth it.

The End